CLOSE TO THE EDGE

Grieving the death of her brother, Alix decides to make a fresh start on the Dorset coast. Her new job, running the tearoom attached to Mellstone Gallery, comes with its own difficulties — not least the petulant attitude of her employer's daughter Saskia. On top of this, Alix soon discovers the feud between her landlady and her neighbours, twins Cameron and Grant. Despite being warned to stay away, Alix is drawn to Cameron's warm nature. With his plans to move north and her turbulent past, could they have a future together?

SHEILA SPENCER-SMITH

CLOSE TO THE EDGE

Complete and Unabridged

LINFORD
Leicester

First published in Great Britain in 2019

First Linford Edition
published 2020

A catalogue record for this book is available
from the British Library.

ISBN 978–1–4448–4459–7

Published by
Ulverscroft Limited
Anstey, Leicestershire

Set by Words & Graphics Ltd.
Anstey, Leicestershire
Printed and bound in Great Britain by
T. J. International Ltd., Padstow, Cornwall

This book is printed on acid-free paper

Cool Reception

Alix wound down her car window and sniffed in appreciation at the fresh Dorset air.

Yesterday she had been standing on a Cornish cliff-top with the surging Atlantic foaming on the rocks beneath, the power of nature she had previously taken for granted but never, until recently, feared.

Now she was here in a pretty inland village many miles away. She loved the scent of grass-scented air and damp soil. There was something about the earthiness of it, the feeling of age and stability that made her feel surprisingly alive and well.

Smiling, she settled down to wait for someone to turn up to meet her here outside One Meadowlands as arranged.

She had found the cottage easily enough, the smaller left-hand one of a pair whose thatch looked unkempt compared with the newness of its neighbour. A *For Sale* board leaning drunkenly towards her looked as if the merest breath of wind would send it toppling.

She was lucky to be able to live in this place until it was sold. One less thing to worry about until she got settled in her new job of setting up and running the tearoom attached to Mellstone Gallery.

'Hilda needs to do something about that board,' a voice behind her said as she got out of the car at last. 'I'd come and fix it myself if I wasn't forbidden to enter the property.'

The man surveying her was at the garden gate next door. His tousled hair looked as if he frequently ran his hand through it.

She spun round.

'Hilda?'

'Miss Hilda Lunt, owner of the property. You're waiting for her?' The look he gave her was penetrating and at odds with his casual appearance. The dark patch on the shoulder of his maroon jersey matched another on the knee of his jeans.

Alix smiled.

'She'll be here in a minute, I expect.' She lifted her bag out of the car. He hesitated for a moment and then vanished as a girl came striding along the lane towards her and stopped abruptly.

'Alix Williams?'

Alix straightened.

'That's me.'

The girl adjusted the strap of her sleeveless top.

'I'm Saskia.'

'Hi, Saskia.' Alix hauled up her bag. It seemed that she was expected to know who Saskia was. Well, she would play along. 'I was expecting Miss Lunt to meet me here.'

'She can't come. I've got the key to the cottage. I've got to show you round. Come on.'

Saskia flicked open the gate and Alix crunched her way behind her up the straight gravel path between low box hedges that were a stern contrast to the rampant disorder on either side.

At the door Saskia turned and scrutinised her.

'Hilda Lunt's got a feud going with him next door and it sometimes gets nasty. She'd have warned you herself but she was rushed to hospital half an hour ago.'

Alix was horrified.

'A fight?'

'Nothing like that. They haven't come to blows yet.' Saskia spoke as if it was only a matter of time.

'Oh.'

'My mum owns the gallery where you'll be working. She's got an appointment she can't break. That's why she can't be here to let you in.'

'I see.' So that's who Saskia was, Jenny Finlay's daughter.

Saskia thrust a key into the lock.

'Right. There's not much room. I'll go first.'

The door opened straight into a living-room with a staircase. Through the open door into the kitchen Alix saw a deep sink and wooden draining board beneath a high window. The back door was half-glazed with a streak of mud on the outside.

Alix hid a smile. A ball of mud expertly thrown from next door by the man she had seen? No wonder he had splashes of something on his clothing. Maybe Miss Lunt had hurled one back? Before her rush to hospital, of course.

'Two up and two down,' Saskia said.

Alix put down her suitcase and placed her bag on the nearest chair.

'Thank you. Is Miss Lunt very ill?'

'No-one knows. She's like that. Bullies everyone else to tell her all their business but clams up about her own. I'm not supposed to say anything but I'd keep my head down if I were you. Cameron Grant owns the other two cottages in the row, converted into one now. He wants to buy this one but Hilda won't hear of it. The best of luck.'

'You think I'll need it?'

'And some.' Saskia flicked Alix an unfriendly glance as she moved towards the door. 'Just be careful, that's all. Mum said she'll call in to see you on her way back from Wernely. You'll find some stuff in the kitchen to get you started.'

And she was gone.

Alix took a deep breath and let it out slowly. Well, she had arrived. Not an effusive welcome. Maybe Saskia's mother, Jenny Finlay, was the same? But time enough to consider that later.

Meanwhile she had a job to do and the sooner she was settled in the better, since she had no choice but to make the best of things. And what did anything matter compared with the last few traumatic months?

She humped her luggage up the narrow staircase and into the small bedroom at the front. At the window set deep in the wall hung flimsy white curtains. This was a surprise and not quite what she expected from the daunting-sounding Miss Lunt.

Stark walls and gunmetal paint on window bars would have seemed more likely and a horsehair mattress on an iron bedstead.

Instead, the room was charming. There was even a faint scent of cloves and dried rose petals from the flowered china dish on the bedside table.

Hope sprang up, unbidden. First she would unpack and then have a look around outside. The ongoing feud had nothing to do with her, even if the situation sounded disturbing.

★   ★   ★

The main part of the garden was in front of the cottage and at the back was a yard paved with ancient weed-riddled stones and bordered by a low stone wall. In one corner was a small ramshackle outhouse. In another was a rusty old mangle that looked as if it hadn't been used for centuries. Near the back door was a wooden seat.

Alix made herself a mug of tea, opened the packet of biscuits she found in the kitchen cupboard and carried them outside through the back door that needed a huge push to get it open.

Here in this sheltered spot the sun was warm on her face. Bees murmured amongst the rambling honeysuckle overhanging the boundary wall but there was no other sound.

The garden next door was probably less utilitarian than Miss Lunt's back yard if the flowering shrubs on the other side of the wall were anything to go by.

Its owner was obviously at home on this sunny afternoon, wearing what had looked like gardening clothes. He could be over there now, working away behind those bushes while listening for the slightest sound from her and planning what to do about it.

But just listen to her! There must be something in the stone cottage wall behind her that was communicating Hilda Lunt's paranoia to her. How ridiculous was that?

Smiling, Alix drank her tea.

A New Start

Stephanotis, Jenny Finlay thought. Now why should that suddenly pop into her head when she had been concentrating on getting the job done as quickly as possible without annoying the new wooden-faced manager of the Roselyn Guesthouse?

She had shown him her portfolio on arrival but he had been patently unimpressed by the photographs of work she had done here over the years.

Ceramics and flower arranging combined might be unusual enough to cause some sort of comment from him, she had thought.

At least he might have looked interested in the one of which she was most proud, a magnificent display of deep orange lily-like alstroemerias on a circular dish of blues and greens. This particular piece of her ceramic work had been one of her favourites and she had hesitated about letting it go.

Placing it on the landing at the guest house filled with one of her flower arrangements had been a good move. Several people had made a point of visiting Mellstone Gallery since to see where she worked on her lovely unique pieces.

'Very well, Miss Finlay,' Wooden-Face had said at last. 'I'll leave you to do a demonstration of your work as a necessary check. No doubt my house-keeper will provide all you need.'

Jenny was tempted to make a sharp retort and tell him where to put his begrudging offer of her contract renewal where it deserved to be, in the compost bin. But good sense prevailed. What did appreciation matter against financial gain?

She wanted to live without money worries. But she was likely to have plenty of those in the future now that Saskia had come home for good, expecting to have a say in the setting up of her tea-room venture at the gallery.

She finished her test arrangement of tulips and bergenia leaves and placed it on the table in the reception hall, then she prepared to set off for home.

First though she must call in at the Meadowlands cottage and check that her new employee had arrived and had been suitably welcomed by Saskia.

★　★　★

Mellstone Gallery was an attractive low building faced with stone that fitted in perfectly with the cottages Alix had passed on her way through the village. Most of those had thatched roofs but this had tiles that looked old and comfortable even though the building was obviously new.

Four years old, her employer, Jenny Finlay, told her when she had called into the Meadowlands cottage over an hour ago.

Jenny had smiled in a friendly way but she. looked exhausted. Her loose smock was crumpled and the jeans looked loose on her slim figure.

'Miss Finlay?' Alix had said uncertainly.

'Jenny, please. It's good to meet you, Alix. It's generous of you to come and help out at a moment's notice. I don't know what we'd do without you.'

Alix felt herself flush.

'It's nothing, really. I'm glad to be here.'

'Thank you from the bottom of my heart. I hope Saskia's been looking after you. I won't come in. Give me time for a shower and something to eat and I'll meet you in the gallery and we can talk then.

'It's easy to find. Cross over the main road by the pub and go up the lane to the Tidings Tree on the green. A bit further on and you'll come to Mellstone Gallery on the left. Shall we say an hour?'

Another brilliant smile and she was off, the sun glinting on her dark hair as she hurried down the gravel path.

The land in front of Mellstone

Gallery was partly paved and marked out with dull red bricks to form parking spaces. To edge the area someone had planted trees that were just swelling into leaf.

On either side of the entrance stood two huge blue pottery containers full of feathery green-leafed plants and white daisy-like flowers. The whole effect was appealing.

Alix hesitated in the open doorway then saw that Jenny Finlay was coming forward to greet her. She looked more relaxed now and the faint blush in her cheeks made her look younger, almost as young as her daughter and twice as friendly.

She smiled.

'Come in, Alix, and take a look around. I'll show you the showroom first and then we'll get down to business.' Her eyes twinkled. 'Alix is a pretty name — is it short for Alexandra? I seem to remember my mother mentioning that on the phone to your friend in Cornwall.'

Alix stiffened. What else had they talked about, those two women, apart from the name her family had always used for her? Her breath rose painfully in her throat but there was no hint of condemnation in the older woman's face.

'Alix, please,' she said, ashamed of her suspicions. It was the name she was going by now although she had never been called it, except by family. A new place, a new job, a new name.

'As you like, of course.' Jenny threw open a glazed door and stood aside to let Alix enter first. 'Well, what do you think?'

She was obviously proud of the showroom. Alix exclaimed in pleasure at the beautiful ceramics displayed on the shelves and tables. Some of them had flowers arranged in them, one with an elegant arrangement of tulips.

Other smaller pots were filled with forget-me-nots and scyllas. They were of myriad colours and designs, some smooth and shiny, others with rough surfaces.

'Pick them up if you want,' Jenny suggested. 'They're meant to be touched, all of them, except the ones with arrangements in them.'

Alix did as she was invited, loving the rough feel.

'This one makes me think of the humpy ground you get on grassy hills.' It seemed an odd thing to say and she hoped she hadn't offended. She picked up another, a smoother one and, turning it over, saw a design of a tree marked out on the bottom.

She saw then that the white walls of the showroom had a hint of green in them and on the desk near the door was a pile of leaflets that featured the picture of a tree above the lettering.

'My logo,' Jenny said. 'It has a lot of meaning for me.'

Alix nodded, wanting to ask the reason but not quite liking to. She sensed something here she had no right to probe. In silence she replaced the pot and picked up another.

'You passed the Tidings Tree on your

way here,' Jenny said. 'I can remember when the branches of the original tree almost touched the thatched roofs on some of the cottages. A favourite spot for artists.'

'Your mother's an artist, isn't she?'

'She had a studio in St Ives at one time but you'll know that. It's where she met your neighbour and boss, of course. Let me show you the room we have here.'

This was next to the showroom, a larger empty space with small tables stacked at one side. There were chairs too in matching wood of a light colour. At once Alix imagined them spaced out with coloured cloths and each with a tiny flower arrangement in charming pots of various shapes and colours.

The sunlight from the wide windows would glint on the cutlery and glassware in a satisfactory way.

Alix smiled.

'This tearoom is new for Mellstone, isn't it? The only one like it?'

'I thought about it for ages before I

decided to go ahead. Coffees served in the mornings and teas in the after-noons. Somewhere for locals to meet and new customers to drop in.

'Light lunches too, perhaps, but that's up to you. I needed someone to get it up and running when I was left high and dry. I was so pleased when your name came up, Alix. And now you're here.'

Jenny flicked some imaginary dust from the window-sill and looked musingly at the tarmac area outside.

Alix followed her gaze.

'Our café was so different. It was the cottage next to ours a few miles out of town with a pretty sheltered garden.' She hesitated, hoping she didn't sound critical. 'We were close to the coast path so we got a lot of walkers. The owner let me take over as manager when she married and moved out.'

'And you did a marvellous job, by all accounts.'

Alix felt warmth flood her face.

'I liked it there.'

'And now you want a change.'

This was said in such matter-of-fact tones that Alix felt reassured. It seemed that her new employer didn't know about the recent events that made her move necessary. Relief flooded through her. She smiled a little uncertainly.

'Cameron suggested we make use of the outside too,' Jenny said.

'Cameron?' Alix was startled.

'He reckons it wouldn't take long to get it paved and he's organising it for us.'

Alix smiled. Us? It sounded good. She was already feeling a part of the team. But Cameron, the man Saskia had come out with who was involved in a feud with her landlady? She wanted to ask more but Jenny was talking.

'The foundations are there. It was the school playground, you know, a long time ago. Cameron's been most helpful. My workshop is the room behind but you won't want to see that now. Come and have a look at the kitchen.'

This, as Alix expected, was the

adjoining room, bright with shining utensils on wall racks and with boxes obviously containing crockery piled on the worktops. A glass door gave access to the outside area from here as well as from the main room.

'So you'll come?' Jenny said, as if there was any doubt.

'Yes, oh, yes. I can't wait to get started.'

Fresh Opportunities

Alix was up early next morning. She opened her bedroom curtains to look out over the dewy garden to the downs beyond, hazy against the pale sky.

It was the peace of the early morning that she had loved years ago as a little girl as she had knelt on her bedroom window seat at home to see the silver line of the sea glinting beyond the wedge of the cliff and the stir of the water as the wind caught it.

But Olaf, yawning as he clattered down the narrow stairs to breakfast in the kitchen and late as usual for the school bus, could never understand his young sister's habit of rising hours before anyone else.

Even as adults when together they ran their own studio-shop in town, they were always late opening up for the summer tourists because Olaf, tall and gangling as he unfolded himself from their van, had been loath to leave his bed.

Now, months later, she felt a familiar catching of breath, a slow building up of tension that made her clutch the window-sill in case the ground gave way beneath her.

Not ground, she thought. Floor. The wooden floor beneath her bare feet was wasn't rough Cornish moorland. She was safe now in a Dorset cottage, inland by thirty miles or more.

As she had watched her brother trudge off across the shaggy ground on that terrible day, with his rucksack dangling from one shoulder, she hadn't known how unsafe Olaf was going to be.

He had stretched too far over the cliff, misjudged the distance, glimpsed a bird he needed to identify . . . no-one really knew.

But she had understood how much it had meant to him. He was eager to prove his worth in his position working in the bird sanctuary up the coast that was important enough to give up their beachcombing life for.

He had loved fashioning the sun-bleached wood into objects of beauty the tourists loved, but not as much as he loved the bird sanctuary.

And it had ended suddenly, so suddenly.

After weeks of trying to cope, she and her father knew that it was the end for them there. The opportunity for her here had been the catalyst for them both. Tenants had been found for their cottage as soon as she had been offered the Mellstone job.

Dad had looked at her intently when it had first been mooted, hesitating about his long-held dream of walking from the south coast to the Fame Islands in Northumberland. But he wasn't about to leave her alone, jobless, in their cottage after the tragedy that had torn their world apart.

'Are you sure about the Mellstone job — quite sure?' he had asked.

'I'll make the most of it, Dad, I promise.' Her smile had felt tight. He needed to get away from Cornwall with an easy mind about her. 'It's an opportunity.'

An opportunity to do something of which he approved. The tenuous connection between Zelda, their erstwhile neighbour, for whom Alix had been working and Jenny Finlay pleased him and that was good.

Alix had never thought of herself as adventurous as she grew up in the shadow of an elder brother whose laid-back lifestyle suited her perfectly. Now was the time to prove she was.

Dressed and downstairs, Alix opened the cupboard door above the sink and found flour and eggs. The butter in the fridge would soften a little if she placed it on a bowl of hot water.

She was glad to have something to do and set to work, guessing the amounts she needed because there were no scales.

Ten minutes later she had a dozen

scones in the oven. At least they were proof of her baking skills, making something out of the sparse ingredients at her disposal. Jenny had made it plain that she wasn't going to be subjected to any test but even so it felt good to be able to prove she was fairly capable.

Pity it was too shaded outside at this time of day to enjoy breakfasting there but it might be too cold anyway. And she didn't want to be seen by the man, Cameron. Not yet.

Living alongside each other meant that she was bound to meet him again before long but not till she was ready. He had looked friendly even if his voice had sounded suspicious. But it could have been her imagination working overtime. Saskia had said that the so-called feud was caused by Hilda Lunt refusing to sell her property to someone who was keen to buy it. But how strange was that?

★ ★ ★

24

To Jenny's surprise, Saskia rose early and was downstairs in the kitchen with the kettle rattling cheerfully on the Raeburn when her mother came in.

'I was going to bring you up a coffee,' Saskia said. 'You should have stayed in bed for another five minutes.'

Jenny smiled as she reached for two mugs.

'Today of all days?'

'What's so special about today?' Saskia frowned as she turned to spoon coffee into the cafetière.

Jenny made no reply. She knew only too well what had brought this on. It wasn't as if she had known that her daughter was coming home jobless before she decided to take Alix on but Saskia in this belligerent mood wouldn't remember that.

Saskia poured boiling water into the cafetière.

'We've got to talk, Saskia.' Jenny pulled out a stool from the breakfast bar and sat with her chin resting in her hands.

'About what?' Saskia sat down, too,

and stared at her mother.

'Alix.'

Saskia said nothing.

'I expect you get to on with her or at least make an effort. She's been through a bad time.'

'And you think I haven't?'

'She's doing me a huge favour. Remember that, Saskia, please. I needed someone reliable and Alix was highly recommended and available.'

Saskia leaped up to get the milk jug, banged shut the fridge door in frustration and spilled some of the milk from the jug in her hand as she did so.

Jenny sighed but said nothing.

She had hoped to be first at the gallery this morning but when she arrived Alix was already there.

'I must give you your own key,' Jenny said as she unlocked the door of the gallery. 'Saskia will be along in a minute. We're expecting a delivery from the wholesalers soon after nine and then I've an appointment at the Downland Guesthouse in Blandford. A

26

prospective new customer.'

'For your ceramics?'

Jenny nodded.

'With luck. I supply businesses on a sale or return basis to use for the flower arrangements they commission me to do for them in situ every week. The idea is for their clients to admire the pots so much they want to buy them. It works sometimes. Quite often in fact.'

'That's good, isn't it?'

'Yes, definitely. And I'll make it clear the flower arrangements and their containers on the tables here are for sale, too.' Her sudden smile made her look years younger.

A surge of energy bubbled up inside Alix. She was eager to get started on setting up the room ready for their first customers.

Saskia arrived two hours later when the tables were all in place and Alix was satisfied with the lay-out. The supplies from the wholesaler had arrived and were stashed away.

'You've done it all,' Saskia said, annoyed.

'It had to be done.'

'If you say so.' Her tone was grudging. 'Mum saw Hilda Lunt last night. They'll be letting her out today. She wants to see you later round at her place.'

'She doesn't waste time, does she?'

Saskia shrugged.

'Mum says I've got to take you there. Be ready at seven.'

'The kettle's on. The coffee'll only take a minute.'

Suddenly it was important that Saskia should join her in a companionable way. A team, Jenny had said yesterday. She had looked, it had to be admitted, a little doubtful. But a friendly and relaxed atmosphere had to work if they wanted to attract customers.

'There are scones, too,' she said, 'and strawberry jam if I can find the tin opener. The jam's come in one of those enormous catering things.' Alix heard herself rattling on but Saskia was looking about in that scornful way that was beginning to annoy her.

Alix took her time making the coffee and sorting out knives and plates. Two scones each to start with and a large dish of jam and another of clotted cream. Seeing this, Saskia smiled and reached for the cream.

'Jam first,' Alix said, passing the dish to her.

'You're very bossy. Mum won't like that.'

Alix hesitated, her confidence waning. She was putting on too much of an act. What did it matter what order their customers chose or even if they consumed the scones with nothing on at all?

She had never minded before — neither had Olaf. Especially not Olaf. He never noticed what he was eating and certainly not what others chose to do.

There was a sound outside and Jenny came in, looking with pleasure at her daughter and Alix enjoying their coffee break together. Or so it must seem to her, even if Saskia was leaning back in her seat and looking bored.

'You've done a great job, you two. Well done! The tables look good like this, don't they?' She looked round, smiling.

'I suppose it makes the room look bigger,' Saskia said.

'And scones, too!' Jenny said as she sat down. She took one and reached for the jam.

'I hope you like them,' Alix said.

Getting to Know You

Alix picked up the envelope on the front door mat. Cameron Sutherland of Two Meadowlands. Sutherland? Cameron Grant? Two Camerons living at the same address was too much of a coincidence, so what was going on? Well, there was only one way to find out.

The front gate next door opened easily. Bees hummed in the flowering rosemary and the summer-smell of freshly cut grass filled her with a strange longing for the unkempt garden at home in Cornwall.

The bell rope on one side of the front door looked startlingly new as if it were there only for show. There was no button to press or any other way means of attracting attention as far as Alix could see. So, no choice.

She clutched the rope, pulled and then stood back expectantly. Silence.

31

She tried again. No-one at home? She could stick the envelope through the letter box and make a run for it. But no letter box. She stared where it should have been. How could there not be a letter box? What was it with this place that made it different from anywhere else?

She was trying to work that one out when she heard a step behind her and swung round to see the man himself smiling at her in much more a friendly way than he had yesterday. He was in nicer clothes, too, even though one cuff of his sweatshirt was beginning to fray. His jeans looked almost new and he had on a pair of pure white trainers.

'Can I help you?'

She held out the letter.

'I think this must be for you. It came to me next door by mistake.' She hadn't thought beyond handing him his property and for a moment felt disconcerted when he didn't take it.

'It's good to meet my new neighbour,' he said, 'and on my own ground too since I'm forbidden to enter yours.'

'Miss Lunt said that?'

'As good as.'

'Really?'

'So you've not met her yet?'

'But I've been warned.'

'Aha! So you've been talking about me already? That's why my ears were burning.'

Confused, she glanced away and hoped the warmth in her face didn't shine like a warning beacon.

'The letter?' she said.

This time he took it and stuffed it into his pocket.

'You're not going to look at it?' she said in surprise. 'It's marked Urgent.'

'Time enough for that later. Welcome to Mellstone and to Meadowlands. Am I allowed to know your name?'

As Alix told him she saw the twinkle in his eyes.

'I thought the letter must be for you but I wasn't sure,' she said.

'Oh?'

'Cameron Grant, Saskia said. Or so I thought.'

'Ah yes. Sutherland is our surname, mine and Grant's.'

'You're brothers?

'Twins. Not a bit alike though. A blessing for Grant.'

'It sounded as if you were one person.'

'Some people think we are just because I've moved in with Grant for a few weeks. Miss Lunt for one. Get an idea into her head and it's there for life. She won't like to think of you fraternising with the enemy.'

'So I'd better go?'

'Not a bit of it. I think we should get to know each other, don't you? I hear you're going to do great things with this tearoom Jenny is keen to get up and running?'

'And you're helping with the paving outside?'

'Like to see what's been done at the back here? I'm considering the same sort of thing for the tearoom. I'd like your opinion.'

Alix followed him inside and through

a narrow passage that led straight through to a door at the back that was partly glazed like her own next door. No mud on it, though. She smiled. Perhaps Hilda's aim was bad.

The garden stretched as far as she could see to an archway in a mass of tall shrubs. One of them had such a profusion of orange flowers that it seemed like a patch of bright sunshine.

Cameron saw her looking at it.

'A kerria. My brother's pride and joy. Do you like gardening?'

Alix shook her head.

'I haven't really done any. I enjoy admiring them, though.'

'Wise girl. Let someone else do the hard work.'

This was said is such an amused tone of voice that Alix laughed.

'It's the paving you wanted to show me,' she reminded him, 'although the garden seems to be worth looking at, too.'

'I stand corrected.'

He looked like a little boy caught out

in some misdeed. There was something about him that she liked, the sensitive turn of his mouth and the feeling he gave that he had all the time in the world for a stranger turning up on his doorstep.

She couldn't imagine why Miss Lunt should object to the Sutherland brothers. Perhaps Cameron had hidden depths, some bad quality that she had not yet discovered.

On the paving beneath their feet fallen petals from the sweet-scented honeysuckle on the boundary wall made an intricate pattern. The stone looked natural and perfectly right, as if it had always belonged in this garden. She could imagine it would look right anywhere.

Cameron took her silence for approval. 'Like it?'

She turned to him, smiling.

'It's beautiful.'

'You're the first person to tread on it. I laid the last stone yesterday.'

She looked down. This was a surprise. He had avoided the modern look by choosing old and irregular stones that suited the age of the building. It had seemed so right that she had stepped out on to it assuming it had been there for years.

'So?' he said. Do you think I should place a similar order for Jenny's place?'

'Oh.' She wasn't used to her opinion being sought. Dad had always known his own mind and Olaf simply didn't care. 'I think Jenny should decide, don't you?'

'You don't like being put on the spot, then?'

Alix smiled. It wasn't up to her to make the decision.

'I'll tell Jenny I've seen it.'

'Then so be it. But now, since you're here, like to see the rest of the garden? All Grant's work, of course. Since his wife died he's thrown almost all his energies into it. He'll be pleased to know you admire it.'

They were walking towards the archway now and through it she could see a winding grass path that invited exploration.

'He's done it all himself?'

'Not my line, I'm afraid. I'm more on the wild side. Now don't look alarmed.' He laughed as he saw her hesitate. 'Botany's my scene. You could say a I'm a conservationist. That's my aim, you see, working with young people to start them on a journey of discovery that can last a lifetime.'

'It sounds good.'

'I'm hoping the Field Studies Council will be impressed at my interview in Yorkshire next week. But I'm boring you.'

'I'm never bored.'

He raised an amused eyebrow at her.

'I go on enough about it to poor old Grant. He'll be glad to see the back of me.'

'You think you'll be successful, then?'

'I'll have to wait and see.' He held back a hanging rambler rose branch for her to pass easily beneath the arch.

On the other side, Alix saw that the grass path meandered through a group of fruit trees and looked well-tended.

The scent of newly mown grass hung on the air. Further on was another arch, this time swathed in early pink clematis blooms.

'That's the end of the garden,' Cameron said. 'He has bright ideas, my brother, but I don't let on that I prefer the wild clematis, travellers' joy. Not yet out in the hedgerows up in the hollow, but it soon will be.'

'And do they have that in Yorkshire?'

He grinned at her.

'They have a lot of good things in Yorkshire and soon a fine new tutor at their field studies centre.'

'You, of course.'

'An intelligent girl,' he said approvingly.

They made their way back.

'I've enjoyed meeting you, Alix,' he said as they reached the back door. 'Thanks for delivering the letter.'

So he hadn't forgotten it? But he made no move to take it out of his pocket. Urgent, it had said on the envelope. She wondered why he didn't think so.

Disturbing Memories

To Alix, expecting something far more impressive of Hilda Lunt's home, Trevose Lodge was a disappointment. It looked as if various owners through the years had stuck bits on here and there in a haphazard way that was neither practical nor beautiful.

Saskia gave two sharp rings at the doorbell and then two more.

'That's a signal we're not enemies,' she said. She pushed open the door and went in. 'Come on, Alix, what are you waiting for?'

'Come in, why don't you?' a voice boomed from someone deep inside. 'And shut that door behind you.'

Grinning, Saskia pushed the door shut with a resounding click.

The passage to the back of the house was long and draughty. The room where more loud instructions were coming from was at the far end of the property.

'We're here to see how you are, Hilda.' Saskia raised her voice. 'She's a bit deaf so you need to speak clearly,' she whispered to Alix. 'This is Alix, your new tenant,' she said, as they entered the over-heated sitting-room.

Alix felt a shiver of apprehension at Hilda's long stare.

Saskia held out the arrangement of grape hyacinths and violas in a small green bowl she had been carrying with great care.

'Mum sent this. I'll put it down over there, shall I?' She looked round for somewhere suitably uncluttered.

'Give it here. I'll hold it.' Hilda's tone was ungracious but Alix noticed that she held it protectively in her lap.

'And Mum wants to know how you are now.'

'Never better,' Hilda said in disgust when they were finally seated in the room that was so warm and crowded that Alix felt slightly dizzy. 'Heart

41

murmur indeed. Whoever heard the like?'

'Certainly not me,' Saskia muttered. 'Not many people would have guessed she has a heart — let alone one that murmured.'

Alix's lips twitched as Saskia raised her voice.

'So what happened, then, Hilda?'

Apparently, the hospital had advised a pacemaker which Hilda refused to consider. A growl started low in her throat but came to nothing and she seemed almost relieved as Saskia talked about Jenny's activities and plans for the tea-room.

Saskia leaned back, a satisfied expression on her face. She dwelt on how much hard work had been done and of how exhausted she felt afterwards.

'And Mum's getting some help to get the back sorted out,' she said.

Hilda drew her thick brows closer together.

'What sort of help?'

'Choosing some suitable paving,

placing an order, arranging for the work to be done. Alix has already had a look at some Cameron likes, haven't you, Alix?'

Alix froze, appalled at what sounded like deliberate provocation.

Hilda's face reddened as she glared at Alix.

Alix froze. What was Saskia thinking? The surprise was that Hilda said nothing although it seemed an effort for her not to do so.

Alix gave a tentative smile, hoping that her landlady would see that she wasn't going to takes sides. Cameron had been friendly and she, liking him, had responded but that was all. One, Meadowlands was the only home she had at the moment and she didn't want to lose it.

They didn't stay long after that. As they let themselves out into the fresh air Alix couldn't help a little shiver.

'Poor Miss Lunt,' she said. 'Living alone in that place.'

Saskia shrugged, unconcerned.

43

'She won't hear of leaving. Mum's tried to make her see sense. She's as stubborn as I don't know what.'

'A mule?'

Saskia snorted.

'As twenty mules or more where Mum's concerned. That's why she won't take any rent from Mum for your cottage.'

Alix was taken aback. There were things going on here she didn't understand. The tearoom must be more important to Jenny than she had thought. Far more important. Extra pressure on herself, then. She took a deep breath that had something in it like panic.

'You had a lucky escape back there,' Saskia said. 'No interrogation. No threats about neighbours. No rules or regulations.' Was there disappointment in her voice?

Alix hesitated.

'Were you hoping there would be?'

'I was looking forward to it.' No smile or any hint she might be joking. That was Saskia for you, Alix thought. She must get used to it.

'But you went to see Cameron?' Saskia added. She sounded suspicious now. 'Any particular reason?'

'We're neighbours.'

'And?'

'I liked him.'

It seemed that this wasn't what Saskia wanted to hear. She frowned.

They said nothing more as they separated. Saskia seemed deep in thought as she waited for a car to pass. Alix had plenty to think about, too.

It occurred to Alix later that it would make sense for Hilda to sell both of her properties and buy something more suitable for herself. But Hilda wasn't sensible. Far from it if she wouldn't consider any suitable offer the Sutherland brothers might make. And that, of course, benefited her lodger. So, Alix thought, she should be thankful.

* * *

The track away from the village led uphill and far as Alix could see when she left the cottage the following day for an evening walk to explore her surroundings.

She welcomed the sudden feeling of freedom as she got higher. It was on an evening such as this that she and Olaf liked to take themselves off beachcombing in the old van. But no, she would not think about that She simply would not.

Was she always going to struggle with these horrific memories? She stopped and took a deep breath. Concentrate, concentrate, concentrate. Easier said than done.

Surrounding her was this pretty countryside, olive-green downs and the hedges on either side of the sunken track. The tall bushes were thick with hazel and white-flowered hawthorn and as she walked on she caught glimpses of the bare hillsides beyond against the fading sky.

She had never noticed the heady scent of the may blossom before. Now it seemed to hang in air that was so calm that not even a blade of grass stirred. A lamb's bleating cry in the distance was the only sound.

On she went, higher and higher, marvelling at the peace and beauty. To find several people in the field through the gap near the top startled her. She hadn't heard them as she puffed up the last incline, but this wasn't surprising because they were engrossed in listening to someone with an open map in his hands. He was tall, his dark head towering above the men and women surrounding him.

He folded the map in a couple of easy movements and stuffed it in the rucksack at his feet.

'And there you have it,' he said, straightening. He smiled round at them all. He looked faintly familiar.

Questions were being asked. He answered, his face shining with enthusiasm. And then the group broke up, the people talking and laughing. She saw three or four cars parked near the junction of the track and the road.

'Hi there, Alix!'

'Cameron!' He must have been there too but she hadn't seen him until now, standing a little apart from the others as if he didn't quite belong.

'Don't look so shocked. This is a public bridleway. A holloway, actually, a deep high-banked track you find a lot round here and centuries old. You've chosen a good evening for a walk.'

'You, too. Or are you with those people?'

He looked round at the disappearing figures.

'Yes and no.'

'You're not sure which?'

He grinned.

'Grant was afraid no-one would turn up on this outing he organised for his lecture group and I was doubtful myself. He gets carried away on a subject he finds fascinating and is desperate to share his knowledge. Then he's full of doubts when it's all set up.

'So I tagged along for moral support, bored out of my mind.'

Alix smiled.

'You don't look bored.'

She could see the family likeness now, the same quirky smile.

'I've let him down, I'm afraid, with my lack of interest in his map-reading skills. I tried not to let it show this evening in the face of all that enthusiasm. Next time they're off to find the source of the Nile. I'll give that one a miss.'

'The Nile?'

His eyes danced.

'Mellstone Brook, if you prefer.'

She smiled too, liking his flight of fancy to get his point across.

'But truly I've had it up to here.'

'And yet you came with him?'

'What better place to be on a fine spring evening?'

She couldn't argue with that but a rising breeze was beginning to stir her hair. She brushed it out of her eyes.

'I should be getting back. I only meant to see where the track led.'

Car doors were banging, engines starting. In moments they were gone.

The sudden silence was stunning.

'We'll walk back together, shall we?' Cameron was looking at her as if he suspected she might refuse.

Alix hesitated for only a moment. She had wanted to be alone, feeling she was not good company this evening. But she liked Cameron and a rebuff would be unkind.

She nodded.

The way down seemed quicker, probably because it was now familiar. This had often happened when she and Olaf were returning home in the van from some expedition. There must be a name for it, Something Law? Homing Law. Something like that.

Cameron let her go ahead of him on the narrower parts. They paused once or twice to look closely at the may blossom so thick it looked as if someone had dotted heaps of snow on the hawthorn bushes and added a shake of pepper for good measure.

'It's a good year for blossom,' he said. 'Did you notice the pear blossom earlier and the plum before that?'

'We didn't have much blossom around us,' she said. 'There's an apple tree in our village but that's about all.'

He looked interested.

'Cornwall, Jenny told me. The north coast?'

'Bare and rugged, you could say.'

'And wildly beautiful.'

She didn't answer, for the sudden longing for home shook her. What was she doing here in this alien place full of strangers? But Cameron didn't seem like a stranger. His easy friendliness had made her feel welcome in Mellstone.

'What was your brother talking about to his group back there?' she asked.

'He looked in his element, don't you think, with all that brandishing of maps, poor chap?'

'You're sorry for him?'

Cameron shrugged.

'The history of cartography, would you believe? Rights of way, map references and symbols. I tell him he's mad.'

'Those people didn't seem to think

so. They seemed so keen.'

'Are you interested in that sort of thing?'

She considered.

'I've never thought about it.'

'Then don't. That's my advice for what it's worth. My father was a keen cartographer, too. He worked for the Ordnance Survey in the old days. Climbed Scottish mountains with a sixty-pound battery on his back, to shine lights across vast areas so the heights of other peaks could be checked. They were pleased when one of us took an interest.'

'Your parents?'

'I was the bad boy, you see. Flowers, plants . . . whatever next? To take it up as a career was the very end. Effeminate to a degree.'

'That sounds a bit harsh.'

Cameron said nothing to that. Instead he picked up a misshapen branch of hawthorn from the grass on the bank.

'Someone's been doing some hacking down. A strange shape, don't you think?'

In an instant she saw it in Olaf's hand

and the expression of concentration on his face as he looked at it and saw things in it no-one else saw. A boat's hull, perhaps, or a decoration for a table.

Alix had tried to view everything they found with Olaf's eyes but could never quite achieve his vision. Fashioned by his expert hand into things their clients appreciated meant that sales were usually booming. Returning visitors had always made a beeline for their shop.

Suddenly the ground was hazy and far too close.

Cameron leaped towards her to support her.

'Hey, sit down for a moment. Put your head between your knees.' The grass on the bank was green and lush. It felt cool, too, and safe. He sat down beside her and waited until she raised her head again. 'Better now?'

She nodded although she couldn't stop shivering and, seeing this, he wrenched off his jersey and put it round her shoulders. Alix stared at the crooked branch in his hand.

'You don't like it?' He hurled it with some force.

'We found things like that on the beaches,' she murmured, 'wonderful shapes of driftwood, old dried up bits of bladder wrack . . . '

'Washed up by the tide?'

She nodded, remembering.

'After heavy storms was the best time.'

'What did you do with them?'

His voice seemed to recede and then grow stronger again. She took a deep breath.

'Olaf made beautiful things from them. My brother. He was clever.'

'A strange sort of hobby.'

'Not a hobby. For real.'

'Really?' His tone was disbelieving.

'We had a shop in town. People bought the things he made.'

'They paid good money? And what was your part in all this?'

'I helped him find things. I helped in the gallery.'

'And you actually earned a living that way?' Cameron was still incredulous.

'We liked it.'

'But seasonal, surely?'

'The winter was a good time for stocking up.'

'Especially for Olaf, it sounds like.'

'Me too.' She was defensive.

'Hardly a sensible career for a grown man playing about with bits of flotsam and jetsam the sea threw up.'

'But you don't understand. Olaf's talent was huge.'

'But wasted on driftwood.'

'He made people see things, think differently.'

'But there couldn't be much future in it.'

'The shop and studio got burned down,' she said.

'Ah! A good way out.'

A moment's stillness. Then Alix threw off his jersey and got up.

'Olaf would never do what you're implying and neither would I.'

Before she knew it she had reached the bottom of the track and Meadowlands was in sight.

How dare he criticise Olaf, who was honest and sensitive and artistic, the finest of men and someone she had looked up to all her life and who had always been there for her since the time she had felt her world, was falling apart when Mum died.

Alix had been playing in the long grass in the front garden at four years old when Olaf had come to find her. She remembered the scratching of a stray bramble on her bare legs and how she had wanted to stop and dab at the blood with her hanky. But Olaf's hand on her arm was firm.

She had felt taut with fear because of his tense expression as they went inside to where Dad was waiting to tell them that Mum had died and that they must be brave and look after each other.

It had been Olaf then who had hugged her tight and had been kind and steady while she was blinded by sobs.

★   ★   ★

Alix was almost in tears now as she reached her gate and let it clang shut behind her. Indoors, she snatched a tea towel from the kitchen rail and held it to her face.

How could she have thought of Cameron as a friend? He was critical and tactless, deliberately obtuse as he trampled on her memories.

Her hands shook as she replaced the tea towel and took a deep breath.

It seemed she could only be safe when she was absorbed in her work in the tearoom. The official opening was in three days' time and she had assured Jenny that all would be well.

Jenny had arranged for her good friend, Cathy Varley, from the farm down the lane, to assist Alix in the showroom for the day and that was good.

Cathy had been introduced to Alix the day before when she had called in to see how things were going. Alix had been charmed by her appreciation of the hard work that had gone into making both the showroom and the tearoom so attractive and welcoming.

'Cathy and I go back a long way,' Jenny had told Alix. 'Ever since I was nine years old when we came to live in Mellstone. Cathy was the infants' teacher in those days in the school and, big as I was, I needed a bit of special attention and she was there for me.'

Alix smiled. It was easy to imagine this kind woman noticing a young girl's need. She would be good at talking to prospective customers at the Open Day, too. All at once a surge of optimism rose in her and she relaxed for the first time since her flight from Cameron.

Soon he would be off for his interview for a job he had high hopes of getting. She hoped he would, too. Let Yorkshire find out what he was really like.

First Day Nerves

Now it was Friday and everything was in place for the gallery and the tearoom's Open Day tomorrow.

Jenny, busy in her workshop, emerged every now and again to remind Alix of some small detail that had suddenly assumed huge proportions. The third time this happened she smiled and shrugged at Alix in resignation.

'You realise what all this is about, don't you? Sheer nerves on my part.' She flicked a spot of clay from her working apron.

Alix knew just how Jenny felt. A horde of butterflies danced inside her every time she thought of the following day.

She needed to prove to Jenny that it was worth her while getting her here and sorting out her accommodation and that it wasn't all a waste of money.

As well, she needed to prove something to herself. And to Dad.

'Don't forget the coffee and biscuits are complimentary all day today,' Jenny said. 'But of course you know that. Sorry.'

'All day, yes.'

'Good girl. Take no notice of me.' Jenny gave Alix a brilliant smile.

The gallery showroom for selling her wares looked magnificent, Alix thought.

Jenny had made sure that every stage of her work was represented, starting with the clay on her potter's wheel. She would be demonstrating the start of the process every hour.

Saskia was to oversee the showroom at all times, with the help of Tess Hartland who loved to help in selling Jenny's wares. To Alix it all looked good but to Jenny's eye it was obviously a different matter.

Jenny was looking critically at the delicate arrangements of primroses in their purple and green pots on the tables.

'Do you think I've done these too early?' she asked.

Alix was reassuring.

'You couldn't have spent as much time on them in the morning, could you?'

'I'll be up at six.'

'Having a relaxing shower and knowing that everything's in place?'

'Have you always been this sensible?'

'No-one's accused me of that before.' Alix frowned, thinking of Cameron and his insinuations as they walked down the hollow the other evening. She had reacted to his opinion of her brother so abruptly he must have been taken aback.

A sound like the snapping of a twig outside startled her now and she was once again on the beach at home with the sun blazing down on their heads as she and Olaf scrutinised each patch of salty seaweed and heap of tarred driftwood.

But it wasn't a snapping twig now, only someone treading on something or other as he made his way to the open patio doors.

Jenny's face cleared.

'Cameron at last. I hope the stone delivery's not planned for tomorrow.'

'It wouldn't be, would it?'

'He said he'd phone before he left. I've been waiting to hear.'

Alix picked up the duster from the windowsill and headed for the kitchen. 'I've just remembered . . .'

She closed the door behind her.

* * *

Afterwards Alix found it difficult to remember every detail about the Open Day. She knew only that it had gone even better than Jenny had hoped.

They were both at the gallery early on Saturday morning and by the time the first visitors arrived they were ready for action. Some came straight into the tearoom while others decided to watch Jenny's demonstration first.

Although the patio doors were wide

open the room soon felt stuffy and overcrowded on this sunny morning. If only the outside area was finished and in use.

Yesterday, when Cameron arrived, Alix had tried to keep a low profile. She had escaped to the kitchen and was trying not to listen to the murmur of voices in the next room. Then the intervening door opened.

'Coffee?' Jenny said in a bright voice. 'In here, I think?'

'Why not?' Cameron had sounded quite at home as he pulled out stools from beneath the table for the three of them.

With her back to them to hide her flushed face, Alix filled the kettle and plugged it in. Jenny had already spooned coffee into the cafetière and was reaching for the mugs. Alix could feel her constrained emotion as she moved swiftly from one job to another.

Cameron talked easily of the route he was planning and how much he wanted to see for himself some of the work being done at the centre. If there was a strained atmosphere he didn't seem to notice, even though Alix found it hard to respond to his friendliness as he sipped coffee and helped himself to the biscuits Jenny encouraged him to sample.

'Mmm, pretty good,' he said, taking another. 'More of your talents, Jenny?'

'As if. No, these are Alix's.'

He raised his eyes to Alix.

'The best I've ever tasted.'

He had eaten three with enjoyment Alix remembered now, smiling in spite of herself. Jenny must have wondered why she was silent and withdrawn but she said nothing when he finally got up to go.

At the door he stopped. The expression his face had softened as he looked straight at Alix and for a moment she had the feeling that he wished to say something more. But then he smiled.

Alix had stared after him, resenting his easy assurance. She heard a car engine spring to life and turned away from the door, shrugging.

It was hard not to dwell on this now as she moved amongst the crowded tables, removing empty coffee cups and making room for the next batch of friends and neighbours to sit down at the cleared tables.

Saskia, floating in and out of the tearoom, was enjoying the attention and the ready compliments on the lightness of the scones and the delicious biscuits. By rights she should be presiding over the showroom with Cathy Varley but she was doing such a good job of welcoming the customers that Alix felt it would be churlish to remind her.

She was relieved when at last Saskia disappeared. The room was thinning out a little now and there was time to relax. Time, too, for a few precious moments to stand at the open patio doors and take in deep breaths of cool air and imagine how this space outside would look in a few weeks' time.

Jenny had already been at work on some large containers for the plants she had on order, trailing lobelia whose soft shades of blue, pink and mauve would be offset by the orange of African marigolds.

'An odd mixture,' Jenny had said, 'but one that actually works. Complementary colours, you see, mauve and orange.'

Alix screwed up her eyes now as she imagined the effect.

Back inside again she saw that Saskia had returned. In her hands was a large cake tin.

'I've brought these,' she said breathlessly. 'One moment. I'll grab something to put them on.'

Others were coming in now, and the tables filling up again. Someone exclaimed in delight as Saskia held out a colourful plate towards them.

'Did you do all these yourself?'

Saskia's smile enveloped them all.

'There are plenty more at home. I couldn't get them all in the tin.'

'A clever girl. A real asset to your mother.'

Alix collected a few empty cups and plates on the largest tray and carried it into the kitchen. It was hard not to feel sidelined when Saskia was here, useless even. Then she told herself she was being silly.

Of course, their clients welcomed Saskia and enthused over her offering of cakes because she was familiar to them while she, a stranger, was unknown.

Alix would work hard and do all she could to keep herself in Hilda's good books for Jenny's sake as well as her own. She suspected that Hilda's sharp tongue hid deep worry about her heart condition, even if she seemed to ignore it.

And one day soon she would hear from Dad and by that time she might have proved herself here and he would be proud of her.

She washed the china with vigour and left it to drain. Then, taking a deep breath, she returned to the tearoom.

An elderly lady, elegant in a green dress and matching jacket, seated herself at a table for two and looked with interest at Alix as she came forward to take her order.

'I'm pleased to meet you at last, Alix,' she said in a low pleasant voice. 'I'm Elisabeth Ellis, Jenny's mother. She's told me a lot about you, of course. All good, I may say. My husband and I have been away for a while or we would have met before.'

Alix smiled.

'Jenny told me. You live at Nether End, don't you, on the lane up to the downs?'

'I hope you'll visit us soon when you're not so busy. I see you're doing well today. There was a good crowd of people watching my daughter at work at her wheel and trade seems to be booming in the showroom.'

Elisabeth placed her order after that and Alix returned with a laden tray.

'Have you a moment to sit down too, Alix?' Elisabeth asked. 'That's a lovely big teapot and all we need is another cup and saucer.'

Alix hesitated for only a moment. Saskia was busy with customers at the big table at the window. It felt good to sit down for a few moments and drink tea with someone who was interested in her well-being and wanting to know how she was settling into Hilda's cottage.

In her turn Elisabeth talked of how Saskia had taken up her place at Exeter University and Jenny had become qualified in the combined art of ceramics and flower arranging.

'It wasn't long after that when Hilda Lunt had her accident along the lane,' Elisabeth said, 'trying to climb over a gate to get into the copse. Luckily, Jenny found her. She'd fallen and broken her arm, poor Hilda. She's been on Jenny's side ever since and against anyone she thinks is doing her down. Loyal to a T.'

'I see.' And Alix did, only too clearly.

'Starting up her business here was hard work, of course, but my daughter's nothing if not determined. Resilient, too. There have been a few knocks along the way, of course. I pray that nothing will happen now to rock the boat.'

By the time Elisabeth got up to go Alix felt relaxed and happier than she had all day.

Again, the room was emptying except for one person seated at a table by himself. For a second Alix froze. Could it be? No, not Cameron. Her twinge of disappointment surprised her but how ridiculous was that when she had resolved to steer well clear of him?

She watched as Saskia approached Grant, smiling.

He looked up at her.

'It's Alix I've come to see. Your mum wants you in the showroom for the next ten minutes, Saskia. She sent me to find you. Cathy needs a break as it's lunchtime.'

Saskia scowled.

'Then what are you doing here, may I ask, Grant Sutherland, sitting here drinking coffee?'

'Not yet,' he said pleasantly. 'I'm waiting to be served. By Alix. Now run along.'

With another glare at him, she swung round on her heel and strode to the door. Alix could imagine it slamming had it not been wedged wide open. She shuddered.

Grant picked up the menu.

'The scones sound good. Jenny recommended them. With cream, of course — and jam, and plenty of it.'

Alix smiled.

'A cream tea before lunch? You'll start a new trend.'

'Too early?'

'Not a bit of it, if that's what you want.'

'I can't think of anything better with you serving it instead of that fiery madam. I'd pay double for that.'

'That sounds fair.'

'And in reward I'd like you to come to a barbecue do at my place on Monday evening. A chance to meet a few people and get to know them. How does that sound?'

'Oh.'

'Oh?'

'I'll get your order.'

Alix made her way to the kitchen. Grant was Cameron's brother, his twin brother at that, and Hilda Lunt's sworn enemy. New experiences were what she was seeking, though. She would be a fool to turn this invitation down since Cameron would be away.

She returned to Grant and set the tray down carefully on a neighbouring table, aware that he was no longer alone. Seated opposite him was a girl of about her own age who smiled at her. Keeping her dark curly hair in place was a wide ribbon. The deep red suited her.

'Another cup?' Alix asked as she finished unpacking the tray.

'She's not stopping,' Grant said. 'Just here to check date and time, that's all. Isn't that so, Michelle?'

'Could be true.' Her eyes danced.

He lifted the cafetière and poured.

'Good coffee, this. I can tell by the rich aroma. Heady stuff.'

Michelle gave Grant a provocative look.

'And I can tell when I'm not wanted.'

Grant grinned.

'Behave yourself, please, Michelle. The barbecue's at eight or thereabouts. I'll expect you early, you and your aunt, to help with the food. Don't be late.'

'As if!'

With a cheery wave, she left.

Grant reached for a scone.

'Seriously though,' he said as he helped himself liberally to jam and cream, 'it could be a lonely life on your own in that cottage of yours. I can't see this tearoom being a hive of industry. The elderly and retired popping in every now and again if you're lucky.' He raised an eyebrow.

'Nothing wrong with that, especially if they bring friends and word gets round,' Alix said.

She wasn't going to be defeated so easily. What was it with Grant and his brother, seeing the downside in every-thing?

Cameron was probably up at that place in Yorkshire finding fault with his surroundings at this very minute. Checking the fire insurance more than likely and making snide remarks about the wonders of false pay-outs.

She smiled.

'We might surprise you yet.'

He reached for another scone and piled it high with jam and cream.

'Coachloads of youngsters on a school trip? Honeymooners spending shedloads of cash in the showroom and then coming in here?'

'Everyone welcome as long as they don't overdo the cream.'

'Touché!' He grinned. 'Delicious.'

He wiped his mouth with the back of his hand, stood up and headed off.

Jenny had come unnoticed into the room and nodded towards Grant's departing figure.

'He'll be inviting you to join one of his walking groups next,' Jenny said when he was out of earshot, 'and a good thing, too. You need time away from here, Alex. You deserve it.'

'Deserve what?' Saskia said, joining them. She looked scornful. 'Not one of Grant's days out, if you can call them that? I wouldn't be you for the world, being bossed about by a know-all like him.'

Jenny picked up a sugar basin and put it down again.

'Go and get the kettle on indoors, Saskia, and be quick about it. We'll follow in a minute. I'll help clear these things first.'

With a little triumphant smile, Saskia left.

'I might even take Grant up on it if you're quite sure I can change my day off?' Alix said, watching her go.

'Not a problem.' Jenny sounded supremely confident.

'But . . . '

'Saskia won't mind one little bit. Look how helpful she's been so far. I'm proud of her.'

Alix hesitated. Jenny hadn't noticed how her daughter had been acting and that was good, wasn't it? Jenny had enough responsibilities of her own without adding more worry.

In any case as the days went on, Saskia and she might be become the team that Jenny already suspected they were.

'And Grant and his brother are being supportive too, aren't they, Alix? We're lucky.'

Here Alix could agree and said so.

Jenny's smile of approval was warming. What had Grant done, Alix wondered, to be so out of favour with Saskia but not with her mother? And with Hilda Lunt as well, if Saskia were to believed.

Saskia had been quick to encourage bad feeling between Hilda and the brothers, almost as if she wanted trouble to be brewing between them with Alix involved in it.

It seemed that Cameron wasn't her only enemy. Saskia was, too.

Secret Fears

'I know so little about cartography,' Alix said. She leaned back in the garden seat and placed her empty plate on the grass beside her. Happy voices rose and fell in the calm air.

Over by the barbecue Grant was enjoying himself enormously, wielding a spatula in one hand and a large fork in the other, deftly turning sausages, chicken burgers and steaks. A haze of appetising smoky smells rose in the air around him.

Michelle gave a happy laugh.

'Join the club. Me, I go along for the company. I like a good laugh.' She threw across to Grant such a challenging look that he put down his cooking implements and came across to them.

'Anything more for you girls? There's loads left and no-one else seems to want it.' He glanced in a despairing way at the people reclining on an assortment of chairs and blankets strewn across the lawn. 'It's all got to be disposed of before my brother gets home.'

'Doesn't he like food?'

'Can't bear waste.'

Michelle shrugged.

'But he couldn't face being here with us lot to help eat it?'

'Not when he's at a job interview in Yorkshire and plans to stay away until the end of the week.'

'Poor chap.' Her voice held a disparaging note.

Alix started to speak and then thought better of it. What did it matter what anyone thought of Cameron's plans when they obviously knew nothing about them? Not that she knew a great deal, of course, but she understood anyone wanting to follow his dream and going for it. That's what Olaf had done, and now Dad was doing, too. And so was she, in a way, if you counted her struggle to do something with her life after what had happened.

She caught a glint in Grant's eye and smiled.

Michelle finished her mouthful and gave a satisfied sigh.

'What sort of job?'

'Tutor at a Field Centre,' he said, 'working for the FSC.'

'Sounds grim. What's the FSC?'

'Field Studies Council. He's always wanted to work in conservation and now is his chance.' Grant sat down heavily on the empty chair next to Alix. 'Best to discuss our own plans, don't you think? The Ridgeway walk on Saturday.'

'I've been telling Alix. Inviting her to come with us.'

'But didn't I hear someone say something about cartography?'

'I saw you at the top of the hollow the other evening with a group of people,' Alix said. 'You were showing them something on the map. Cameron said . . . '

'Ha, Cameron! So you're the girl my brother walked home? I see everything now, the sly so-and-so. But never mind maps.' He waved his arm expansively and Alix saw Jenny talking to a couple over by the archway. Her hands were down by her sides and she looked out of place somehow.

'An interesting walk on Saturday,' Grant was saying, 'that's the priority. Maps not required where we're going. Do you good, Alix.'

'But I've never been on any long walks.'

'Neither have some of the others. You'll be in good company.'

'That's a matter of opinion,' Michelle said darkly.

'Don't put Alix off. It's going to be interesting. I'm planning a walk along the South Dorset Ridgeway. A bit of a drive first, transport provided. We'll eat at a suitable hostelry afterwards. It's in an area of one thousand ancient monuments.' He spoke with satisfaction but Michelle was horrified.

'One thousand?'

He smiled kindly.

'Don't worry. We shan't be visiting every one of them. We'll see signs of the burial mounds in the distance, that's all. Saturday at ten,' he said. 'Meet down near the pub. So will you come with us, Alix?'

She hesitated.

'The south? But doesn't that mean it's near the sea?'

'Parallel with the coast but not very near. And we'll only be walking four or five miles max. You can manage that?'

'Stop it, Grant, you're pressurising her.'

'Jenny! You crept on me.'

'Just want you to know that more guests have arrived. Starving, I gather.'

Grant leaped to his feet.

Jenny's half-smile vanished as soon as he had returned to his duties and Alix noticed her pallor.

'Are you all right? I mean . . . '

'Maybe I'll go now. Grant won't mind.'

'Shall I come with you?'

'No, no, stay here. I'll be all right, really. It's not far.'

Alix sank back in her seat but as she

watched Jenny slipping away she thought of the planned walk. It would be parallel with the sea, an inland walk. But how far inland? She would consult the map when she got back.

She had assumed that she would be quite safe in Mellstone from the evocative sounds and smells that reminded her so vividly of her Cornish home. Waves lapping the shore, raucous sea birds sweeping the cliffs and the tang of seaweed.

Grant had looked surprised when she mentioned the sea and so it wasn't uppermost in his mind. And neither should it be in hers.

★   ★   ★

The laughter and voices became fainter as Jenny walked along the lane, heading for Marigold Cottage. Home, where she could immerse herself in her latest designs for her ceramics. But not this evening, for even there she would still hear Cathy Varley's daughter's voice in her ear telling her that they had fixed a date for their wedding and asking her to do the flowers.

In the hawthorn hedge a bird was singing. A happy song that could normally lift Jenny's heart on such a lovely evening. But not this one.

Oliver.

She hadn't thought of Oliver Varley, Cathy's son, for ages. On his few leaves from his charity work in Africa she had made sure to be away from Mellstone. Apart from the first one, of course, when he had returned on a visit as promised for her final answer.

Oliver Varley was twelve years her junior, on the brink of setting off for Burkino Faso, and she knew that remaining in Mellstone and struggling to make a success of her new business venture was the right decision for her and so she had let Oliver go. They had been an item for ages before things came to a head.

A sudden vision of his father's reaction when he had discovered their sordid affair, as he had called it, filled her mind. Ralph Varley, farmer and stalwart of the belief that son should follow father down the generations. He had come to terms at last with his son's wish to spend his life in a god-forsaken place.

He considered himself a fit man still, with years to go before he retired. Oliver might come to his senses by then, with sons of his own to carry on the family farm. But not if he married Jenny, who was unable to have any more children.

And now Oliver and his family would be coming home for his sister's wedding.

Planning Ahead

Walking boots ... yes, no problem there. Alix looked at them appraisingly and tried not to think of the last time she had worn them to do some beach-combing after a sudden storm. A small rucksack even, just the thing. They had never bothered much with waterproofs, she and Olaf, but she had bought herself a rain-proof jacket before coming to Mellstone and that would have to do. In any case, the forecast was good.

She had never walked in a group before and as she crunched down the gravel path her footsteps sounded deafening as if warning her that it was all a dreadful mistake. But that was the old Alix, she reminded herself, living in Olaf's shadow.

Outside the gate she took a deep breath and noticed for the first time that the *For Sale* board had gone. Her thoughts flew to her landlady. Hilda had seemed to enjoy the tearoom Open Day last Saturday and she had been in again twice since then, looking suspiciously through the patio door at the cleared area outside.

Saskia had been there on the second occasion but had kept out of Hilda Lunt's way, smiling at her only briefly before making a clatter of washing up in the kitchen.

Saskia would be there on duty all day today too. Not without protest, of course, but Jenny had been adamant. For a moment Alix wished she could be there in familiar surroundings doing something useful. But this was part of her new life, too, and should be embraced without fear.

She squared her shoulders and set off for the meeting place.

★ ★ ★

The monument on its hill was faint at first in the distance but by the time the minibus with Alan as its driver got closer Alix could see how impressive it was, like a finger pointing to heaven. Maybe that was a bit fanciful but it showed up for miles around.

She could see that Grant couldn't resist imparting information about it when Alan stopped the minibus for them all to pile out.

They were just below the summit here and had a strange view of Hardy's monument because from this angle it was half-hidden by some rising ground between them, but it still appeared impressive.

They gathered in a group round Grant.

'No, not the writer Thomas Hardy,' he said when Michelle asked. 'No relation as far as I know. Sir Thomas Masterman Hardy. He was Admiral Nelson's flag officer on the *Victory* but also served unofficially as captain of the fleet.' He paused and looked sternly at Michelle. 'You've heard of the battle of Trafalgar 1805, I take it?'

Michelle giggled.

'Just about.'

'He was at Nelson's side when he was fatally shot.'

'Kiss me, Hardy?' Michelle said, her eyes wide with interest. 'Isn't that what Nelson said?'

Grant frowned.

'Kismet. Kismet, Hardy. Fate. The end. That's what I think Nelson said and I'm sticking to it.'

Other people murmured their agreement. Grant smiled.

'The monument was erected here on Black Down Hill in his memory by public subscription. It's impressive, don't you think? Twenty-two metres high.'

'But why was it built here?' someone asked.

'He'd lived nearby and his family owned the Portesham estate. They chose this site because they wanted a monument that could be used as a landmark for shipping. From here it's visible for a hundred kilometres.'

Startled, Alix looked towards the

south but saw no sign of the sea from where they were standing. Reassured, she put her arms through the straps of her rucksack and hoisted it up.

Grant picked up his own much larger one.

'Ready for off, then?'

He led the way further up the narrow road from where they had the full benefit of the monument on their left and beyond it the distant sea. Alix felt a familiar stab of apprehension at seeing it there. She looked quickly away.

The lane led downhill for a short distance but soon they had left it and were walking along a grassy ridge with the land sloping down on either side. This was as easy going as Grant had promised and Alix found she was enjoying the feel of soft ground beneath her feet and the soft westerly breeze on her face as long as she resolutely kept her face turned away from the distant sea to the south.

As well, she trained her thoughts on the gallery tearoom back there in Mellstone and the crowds who had flooded it on the Open Day. She had loved seeing the people enjoying the scones and biscuits she had made. They'd liked Saskia's cakes, too, and the compliments had flown. The looks Saskia had thrown at Alix were triumphant.

Afterwards Jenny had thanked them both for their help but had seemed strangely quiet. By that time Saskia had vanished, pleading exhaustion. Jenny, seeming not to notice, had remarked on the numbers of their friends and neighbours who had turned up to wish her well.

'Due to you too, Alix,' she said with a brief smile. 'But . . . ' She broke off and shrugged.

At once Alix understood.

'You mean . . . everyone who came today knew you? There were no strangers? Oh, I see.'

'That's about it. One couple I didn't know, but that's all.'

Alix had bitten her lip, considering.

'We need local people coming in regularly to the tearoom to keep things going,' she said slowly, 'but we need to attract others, too, from further afield or on holiday who'll discover your showroom full of lovely things they can't resist. They'll recommend us to their friends who'll come too and pass the word on. Good publicity.'

'I must advertise more,' Jenny had said.

They had left it at that but now Alix thought of it again. The tearoom would be good for Jenny's business only if it were successful and it was her responsibility to make it so. That's what Jenny needed her for. That little bit extra that Zelda had promised.

She needed to start offering light lunches as well as morning coffee and afternoon tea. Homemade soup and rolls, of course, but something else that the gallery tearoom became noted for and drew people in. To call it a tearoom was a misnomer, for a start.

At home in Cornwall their fish, all silvery and gleaming, were fresh from the sea. Walkers on the cliff path had come to investigate and soon it was a well-known venue, so different from the usual seaside cafés.

They had offered something different yet suitable for coastal Cornwall in rain or shine.

Flotsam Follies was different, too, and the summer visitors loved it. She thought of the day when the rain was battering the window pane at their place in town — a sudden downpour that had sent the tourists scampering for shelter into the gift shop next door and the café down below.

Two had come into Flotsam Follies, a man and woman in shorts and hiking boots and with streaming hair. They looked as if they considered the heavy shower a huge joke. She had smiled at their exuberance.

Olaf had come up from his workshop just then, holding his latest creation, a sailing dinghy speeding before the wind with its sails out on either side. Blue ones. She'd found that material on the stall in the market and had spent all

Saturday afternoon in the workshop working on them until she had got them just right and Olaf was satisfied.

'I can't believe you made it out of rubbish you found on the beach, young man,' the man said. 'Well done.'

'Oh, John, we must have it!' the woman exclaimed in pleasure. 'He's so clever.'

And so Olaf was. Alix had always known that. After the fire she had admired the way he had immediately taken on the position at the seabird place up the coast and immersed himself in it with the enthusiasm he had previously shown for his works of art. He had courage, her brother, and she was proud of him.

Then she blinked and was back again on the South Dorset Ridgeway walking behind a group of strangers on grass as soft as the sand on the beach. Grant, noticing, came back to join her.

'Beautiful, isn't it?' he said. 'I've always loved it up here, being able to see into the distance over land and sea.

Cameron has, too, even more than me, I think. I'm still trying to get my head round him willing to leave it and go off and work in the north.'

'There are open spaces there, too.'

'But not the same.'

'Of course it's not the same,' she said.

'Our country's like that, different wherever you are.'

He looked at her with interest.

'You've travelled a lot?'

'Well, no,' she admitted. 'Not at all. I've read books, pamphlets, that sort of thing. I always liked geography at school.'

'Cameron, too. Nature programmes as well. And geology later on. That's where we differed. But surely the sea is much the same everywhere even if the land isn't?'

She glanced involuntarily to the south. They were approaching the village of Abbotsbury now and that grey line of sea was still there. The same, yet different? In her ears imaginary waves crashed against the granite cliffs of north Cornwall. She shivered.

Grant raised his voice to attract everyone's attention.

'This is where we leave this path and head down to the road. The ruined chapel up there on the hill on the other side is our next port of call.'

There was a murmur of approval and interest. It was easy to see where they were going and Grant let the others go ahead. He rejoined Alix as she hung back a little.

'Are you feeling all right?' Grant's tone was anxious. 'We'll have a bit of a rest when we get up there. You're looking pale, Alix.'

She tried to smile.

'Maybe I'm just hungry. I've been thinking of food, trying to think up a signature dish for the lunch menu at the tearoom to attract people in. It's hard. It needs to be local, you see.'

'No good suggesting my brother's favourite dish, then.'

She was immediately interested.

'So what's that?'

'Yorkshire drop. He'd eat it every day if he got the chance.'

'I've never heard of it,' she said, smiling.

'I don't think many people have. In fact I suspect he made it up to annoy me. He makes batter and drops fruit into it as he pours it in to an ovenproof dish. It tastes good, though.'

As they reached the road at the bottom Grant glanced at her with an intent look that rivalled his brother's.

'I can't believe that hunger is making you nervous, Alix, or even tiredness, when you know we'll be eating soon. First, though, we'll take a look at the ruined chapel. We'll see the swannery from up there on the hill, and the Fleet. That's the expanse of fresh water with the sea beyond on the other side of the Chesil beach. All those thousands of swans milling about. Worth a visit another day.'

All at once her obsession seemed absurd but how could she confide her sudden fear of the sea when it was still distant?

They were walking along a track now, heading for the green hill with the chapel on the top.

As they began to climb, Alix tried to concentrate on swans, elegant white creatures in V formation flying against the sky.

She heard Grant's voice as if from a distance.

'Michelle's playing the fool as usual. What's wrong with that girl? She can't take anything seriously.'

Michelle liked a good laugh, Alix thought, but she wasn't laughing now. She had climbed on to some sort of obstruction and the next moment had fallen. Then she sat up, and held her head between her knees.

Unexpected Rescuer

At once they rushed forward and Alix was down at Michelle's side.

'Are you all right, Michelle?'

Michelle looked up, white-faced.

'I fell.'

'Have you hurt yourself?' Grant's voice was gruff with concern.

'I felt dizzy, that's all. I'll be all right in a minute.' Someone pulled out a flask and poured a hot drink. The colour was returning to Michelle's cheeks now as she drank. Then she struggled to her feet, supported by one of the men.

'See, I'm perfectly all right now. Look, I can move my arms and legs. Nothing wrong with me.'

But Grant looked grave. He pulled out his mobile phone. Alix, watching, heard him explaining to someone what had happened and asking for assistance.

'You're still in the area? Good. I need you to drive someone home. Yes, as soon as you can. We'll wait outside the hall in the centre. You can't miss it.'

'I'll come, too,' Alix said, her voice firm.

To her surprise, Grant made no objection. He sent the others on to visit the ruined chapel on the top of the hill and to continue down the other side on to a footpath and so back to the village to the pub where they were booked in for lunch.

'I'll see you there,' he said. He then turned his attention to Michelle. It was some moments before he suggested they set off, taking it easy as they went down the hill.

'But I'm all right,' she protested. 'You don't have to come, Grant. Go back to the others. I'm OK with Alix. You can see I'm not hurt.' She leaped up and down waving her arms to prove it.

But Grant took no notice until they arrived at the meeting place. With difficulty, Alix managed to persuade him then that she and Michelle should wait on their own while he joined the others.

'Very well.'

'It'll be Alan in the minibus,' Michelle grumbled to Alix as they perched on the low wall to wait in the intermittent sunshine. 'He'll think I'm a right idiot.'

'Then we'll be driven there in style.' Alix moved to get into a more comfortable position on the wall. Only then did she remember her rucksack left behind on the hill. Oh, well, someone would bring it.

'I'll let Alan believe I'm the injured one, if you like. Look, how's this for proof?'

She leaped up and wobbled up and down in an exaggerated way.

Michelle giggled.

'You wouldn't even get a part in a pantomime.'

'No? I won't bother to audition, then.'

They were both laughing when a

Range Rover came around the corner and pulled up beside them.

Cameron? Alix hung back, confused, while Michelle did the talking all in a rush so that her words tumbled over each other. Cameron held his hand up in protest.

'Then you're the injured party, Michelle, I take it? I'd begun to wonder.'

Michelle was outraged.

'Grant seemed to think I was but I'm not. I just got a bit dizzy. And Alix has got to come with me.'

'I insisted,' Alix said hurriedly. 'I wanted to.'

'Better jump in, then, and I'll do my best to be friendly.'

It wasn't until they had got themselves inside and belted up that Alix began to feel herself in the wrong. There was something about Cameron's swift appraising look that made her feel guilty. He must have seen them convulsed with laughter as he drew up.

Michelle, seated beside him in the front, was still complaining about Grant jumping to conclusions.

Cameron was non-committal.

'He feels responsible.'

'That's rubbish.'

'If you say so.'

'Alix is so kind. She knew she'd be missing the meal and everything.'

'Then you're both starving?'

'Of course. Why wouldn't we be after miles of walking?'

'I'd better get you home quickly.'

He put the vehicle into gear, reversed with expertise and they set off. Alix heard the smile in his voice and saw the line of his shoulders relax now that they were on their way.

'I've been stupid, haven't I?' Michelle said. 'Grant must be really fed up. I feel so bad about Alix. If only you could take her back to join the others. They were going for lunch. There'd be time, wouldn't there?'

In the back seat, Alix froze.

Cameron raised his eyebrows.

'Thirty miles?'

Michelle looked so deflated that Alix

felt sorry for her. Grateful, too, of course, for unknowingly getting her out of a difficult situation. She found her voice.

'It's all right, Michelle, I don't want to go back. Really.'

'You heard her,' Cameron said. 'Now go indoors. Your aunt will be home, I take it?' Nodding, Michelle went.

★ ★ ★

'This isn't the way to Meadowlands,' Alix said when they started off again and she had changed to the front passenger seat on Cameron's insistence.

'Well spotted.'

'But why . . . '

'You don't like the scenery?'

She glanced out of the window at her side at the fields and hedges slumbering in the moist afternoon. Before she could say more, he spoke again.

'Just a mile or two to a place I know.'

'But I thought we were going straight home?'

'I haven't eaten for hours and I'm

ravenous. You don't mind?'

Put like that, the detour sounded reasonable and Alix could hardly refuse. They turned off the Hilbury road and took a winding lane that lead downhill for what seemed miles.

The Peacock Feather was a thatched country pub. Cameron parked in the shade of a sycamore.

'This'll do,' Cameron said. 'They do a wonderful curry here. Good and sensible fare. Just what you need, Alix. Come along.'

'Curry?' she said, hesitating.

'A groaning specials board. You'll see.'

He led the way inside to a low-beamed room hung about with copper and brass and with enticing cooking smells vying with the scent of honeysuckle from the vase on the bar counter.

There were low wooden tables and a menu board that promised such delicacies as toad in the hole and mushroom stroganoff. The murmuring voices from the other people in the room was soothing.

They chose to sit near the window looking out at the garden at the back where a water feature sent up a silver spray near a bed of tulips against the far wall.

'A strange name for a pub, the Peacock Feather,' Alix said when Cameron had placed their order at the bar for shepherd's pie for her and chicken curry for himself.'

'No peacocks in the garden?'

'Or anywhere else.'

'You notice names of pubs?'

'I'm trying to think up a good name for the tearoom. We want it to be more than just that. Lunches as well.'

'Feather Gallery?'

She shook her head.

Cameron looked thoughtful.

'The Crystal Fountain. Why not? It has a good ring. It's memorable. Mellstone Fountain?'

'Definitely not. They'd imagine a volcano erupting beneath Mellstone Brook.'

'The Fountain Gallery, then?'

She shook her head.

'Something more sensible.'

'Mellstone Grill?'

'Now you're being ridiculous.'

'Ridiculous, am I? Not more ridiculous than pretending it was a sacrifice on your part to leave Grant's walk.'

She stared at him, surprised. She had been enjoying their repartee but now she was reminded of something she would rather forget.

'Are you clairvoyant?'

'I'd like to think so.'

'Smug, anyway.'

Just then their food arrived and it smelled enticing. She hadn't realised how hungry she was.

'It was the sea, you see,' she confided in a rush of confidence. 'I used to love it but not any more. I could see it in the distance today. It reminded me . . . '

'But isn't that a good thing, memories?'

She shivered.

'Not mine, not those. Suddenly I wanted to be away from it. Someone had to be with Michelle. I thought I was the obvious person.'

'Grant takes these things seriously. He must have been relieved someone was offering.

'I think he was.'

Cameron was eating his curry with evident enjoyment and she had a sudden vision of him seated at a picnic bench outside the café at home with Zelda ducking over him like a mother hen.

'You're smiling, Alix.'

'Just thinking.'

'Of the past?'

Her smile vanished.

'There I go again, putting my foot in it.' He put down his fork. His stillness was disturbing. Her heart softened. This was a serious moment and one she hadn't expected.

'You implied that Olaf would cheat the insurance people,' she said. 'He would never do anything so dishonest.'

'Any more than you would?' There was short pause while he picked up his fork again. 'I never met your brother. I

107

wish I had. But why should my opinion have mattered?'

She felt her cheeks glow.

'I don't like being on bad terms with anybody. You see, if you thought that about Olaf it would have condemned me, too, because it must seem that I agreed to the deception.'

He looked troubled.

'Let me tell you something.' She gazed at him in silence. 'imagine Grant and me, small boys of perhaps six or seven,' he continued. 'Grant was the bright one, good at games, too. I wanted to shine as well but the only way I could be noticed was to come out with some outrageous remark, horrible child that I was.'

'And did it work?'

'I thought it did. I thought I'd grown out of it but it seems I haven't. A weak excuse, I know.'

She smiled.

'But you can't come up with a better one?'

He looked rueful.

'I can't come up with a suitable name for the tearoom, either.'

'Perhaps it will just occur to you,' she said, happier now. 'Things just happen sometimes. Like curry. Fish curry. Someone had a good recipe and we tried it out with fresh mackerel and it worked. And when it was right for Zelda to move away she left me in charge. I knew what to do by then.'

'That was after the fire?'

She nodded.

'Olaf got the job at the bird sanctuary.' She paused. For the first time talking about it seemed right, a relief even. 'And then he fell.' She gulped, took a deep breath. 'He died.'

'And you decided to come to work for Jenny?'

She was immediately on the defensive.

'I wasn't running away.'

'I'd never think that.' His voice was soft 'You're a brave girl.'

'That just happened as well. Dad was ready to move off and we heard of this job in Mellstone. Jenny's mother is my ex-boss's friend, you see.'

'Convenient.'

She was pulled up short. Too convenient? Her face felt hot.

He looked at her in concern but there was no condemnation in his glance, not even when she told him that Dad liked being on his own and didn't feel the need to keep in touch with her.

'That's good, isn't it?' he said.

She looked at him in surprise.

'Good?'

Seeing her reaction, he smiled.

'It leaves you free to get on with your life, branching out on your own, doing what you want.'

She frowned, unconvinced. What did she want when it came down to it? To do well at something to win Dad's approval, of course. How juvenile was that?

She needed to feel needed and she was hardly that when Saskia was around, only too willing to take over the tea-room if she got the chance. She was great at making cakes but how would she be with things like curries — fish ones, for instance?

Not that fish curry would be a good thing to have on the menu with those strong smells seeping everywhere. No, she must think up something really good and different that would make the gallery tearoom the focal point for miles around.

Cameron finished his curry with a flourish.

'Brighter now, Alix? I said something right for once?' His eyes glittered at her.

'I was thinking,' she said.

'I'd noticed. The look suits you. That lovely pensive expression with your mouth curved into a half-smile. Am I allowed to know your thoughts?'

She laughed.

'I was thinking about menus to make the soon-to-be-renamed tearoom a huge success?'

'It means a lot to you?'

'Almost as much as your place in Yorkshire does to you.'

For a moment his eyes looked dreamy.

'We feed people as well,' he acknowledged. 'But there are other things of value we do.'

She wasn't going to let him get away with that.

'Yes? Like at our place, don't forget. Just think of Jenny's showroom for her lovely things. Creative things that people appreciate and buy that bring them happiness.'

He leaned back in his chair and smiled.

'We give things away that you can't see. We open young eyes to the beauty and healing power of nature, inspiring self-confidence, a belief in their own worth when they had none before.'

'You sound as if you're working there already.'

He looked at her in surprise.

'I do, don't I?'

There was a heavy silence and then he smiled again, relaxing. They had finished their meal now but she liked sitting here and had no wish to move which was surprising in someone who had come here with such reluctance.

'I'll get coffee,' he said.

She had seen another side to Cameron these last few hours, a sensitive one but at the same time someone who could see deep into the heart of the matter.

It hadn't occurred to her before that sympathy might have been responsible for the job at the gallery becoming hers.

'Something wrong?' Cameron's voice made her jump.

'Wrong?'

He placed the tray he was carrying on the table and as he did so his phone chirruped.

'Grant? Yes, all correct. Her aunt was there. The Crystal Feather.' He raised one eyebrow at Alix. 'You haven't? The Peacock Grill then. No, I have it. The Peacock's Feather . . . Oh, he's cut me off.'

He sounded so aggrieved that Alix laughed.

'That's better,' he said, smiling too.

She reached forward to pour the coffee.

'It's kind of you to treat me to everything,' she said rather hesitantly. 'I'd like to repay you but I don't know how — unless you'd like me to cook you a meal at home?'

'My dear girl, you're welcome. I was glad of your company, to tell the truth. I've had a bit of a blow.' He hesitated for a moment, looking awkward. 'I just heard this morning that they don't want me at the centre until two weeks after the original date. Something to do with reorganisation that's come out of the blue. They were very apologetic, of course, but there it is.'

She could see that he was bitterly disappointed. His future lay in the north and he was more than ready to go. His light-hearted banter previously was a cover-up for his true feelings and he had done it so well. She would never have guessed here was anything troubling him.

'And Grant wants me out,' he said.

'Surely not?'

'Friends of his from Australia need accommodation, apparently.'

'And they're more important than you?'

Cameron shrugged.

'We understand each other, my brother and I.'

'So, what will you do?'

'Wander off somewhere, I expect. Plenty of places in England to see. But there is something you could do for me, Alix. How about coming with me to a talk I'm interested in? Hilbury Town Hall on Monday evening? Nicer than going on my own.'

Her heart leaped. She smiled.

'On condition you come up with a brilliant name for the tearoom by then.'

'Done.'

Alix had much to think about on the way back to Mellstone.

Angry Encounter

On Monday evening Alix was ready in good time and they arrived in Hilbury soon after the doors opened at the hall and found seats in the middle of the second row. People poured in behind them and the murmur of voices rose and fell.

She looked at Cameron carefully. What was he thinking? It was hard to gauge. He looked perfectly at ease as he leaned back in his seat with his eyes half-closed. The setting sun streaming in through one of the low windows was full on his face.

His eyes had lit up briefly when he saw her waiting for him outside her gate dressed in her light skirt and blue jacket. Her confidence-inspiring clothes, she thought, comfortable, too. His invitation had sounded friendly and casual. Small Wood Management in the Community. Hardly a romantic date, but she needed to feel her best.

Soon there was an expectant hush as the speaker, a small man with a bushy moustache, was introduced as Professor Silken-Grey.

As he began to talk, the electricity in the room mounted. Alix could hardly believe this was the same unobtrusive man who had shambled on to the stage moments before. The screen behind him came to colourful life with woodlands throughout the seasons and the wildlife to be found therein.

Afterwards there was no question and answer session because the professor had an important date to keep and needed to hurry off. A disappointed sigh greeted this announcement until they were told that he had agreed to come again in a few weeks and bookings were being taken in the foyer on the way out.

'Too late for me,' Cameron murmured as they began to make their way out.

It seemed natural for Cameron to offer his hand to guide her through the chattering groups until they came face-to-face with Hilda Lunt.

They stopped, frozen.

Hilda was the first to speak.

'You!' she said, looking at Alix and sounding totally disgusted. 'I saw you both. You didn't see me.'

Her accusing tone seemed to bring Cameron to life.

'Should we have done?'

His hand was still warm on Alix's arm and she wasn't going to brush it off. She made an effort to smile.

'Did you enjoy the lecture, Miss Lunt?'

'Lecture? What lecture? It was a load of old rubbish.'

'Interesting, informative, a good speaker,' Cameron said.

'You disagree with me about that, too?'

'So it seems. Come, Alix, we're blocking the way.'

They left then and it wasn't until they were outside that Cameron dropped his hand.

'Dreadful woman.'

Alix was still shaken but she tried to put the encounter out of her mind as Cameron seemed to have done. Not so easy, she thought as they waited to cross the road to the car park.

'I wonder how she's getting home?' she said.

'Who, Hilda?'

'I know she doesn't drive.'

He sighed.

'You're as bad as my brother, arranging lifts for people who don't want them.' His voice sounded accusing.

She frowned.

'I'm worried about her.'

His eyes shone in the light from the street lamp.

'Wait here.'

He was gone only a short time but she had moments to realise that this might be the last opportunity for being on her own in Cameron's company and she had blown it by her impulsive words.

He was back now, looking jubilant.

'Mission unaccomplished,' he said. 'Refused point blank and I got a mouthful from an irate woman.'

'But how is she getting home?'

He gave a disbelieving snort.

'You won't believe this.'

'Try me.'

'With our friendly speaker. Silky, she called him. Professor Silken-Grey no less.'

'Wow!'

'I was stunned, too. I thought she was joking, fool that I was. Come on, let's go.'

The traffic had cleared now and crossing was easy.

'Home?' Cameron said as they set off.

'Yes, home.'

'You did well back there in the hall, not letting Hilda get to you.'

'I was a churning mass inside,' she confessed.

'You hide your feelings well.'

And she had plenty of those, she thought in sudden pain. She was spoiling the drive home by worrying about Hilda's reaction at seeing them together.

The dark countryside was passing swiftly and all too soon they reached the first houses of the village.

'That awful woman,' Cameron burst out as he drew up outside Meadow-lands and yanked on the handbrake.

Alix said nothing as they got out of the car. She raised her eyes to the night sky, fighting back tears. Hilda had ruined the atmosphere between them as surely as she would have done if she had been sitting stolidly in the back seat.

Cameron slammed shut his door. His footsteps sounded loud in the quiet lane.

'That's it then, Alix. Thank you for an enjoyable evening.'

She took a deep breath as she clicked on the torch on her phone.

'I enjoyed it, too.'

'It's one I shall never forget,' he murmured.

He waited until she had closed her

garden gate behind her and strode up the path with her head held high. No tears now, just a deep lurch of disappointment about something she had no reason to expect.

*   *   *

The banging of the front gate and the crunch of gravel next morning alerted Alix to the approach of someone who obviously meant business. Hilda Lunt, of course. Who else?

With a bunch of parsley clutched in one hand, Alix straightened and stepped over the low box hedge on to the path. She had expected this visit and as she had been unable to settle to anything indoors on this lovely fresh morning, she had decided to do something about the overgrown foliage in the front garden.

Hilda, glaring, came to a full stop.

'You were in Hilbury with him!'

'Well, yes. Cameron invited me, you see.'

'Too weak to refuse, I suppose?'

Alix felt a flush covering her face.
'Why should I?'

Hilda seemed to swell with fury. This couldn't be good for her in her fragile state of health.

'Miss Lunt, please . . . ' She took a deep breath. 'Come inside, please, and rest for a bit.'

To her astonishment, Hilda nodded.

Alix pulled out one of the kitchen chairs and sat down at the table opposite her. She had placed the parsley in the sink and the strong herby smell floated in the increasingly chill air.

Hilda sniffed.

'You found my herb bed.'

Another accusation about a bunch of parsley? Hilda could have a dozen bunches if she wanted. But Hilda, surprisingly, seemed to have little else to say for the moment and her high colour had subsided a little now. Would the offer of a cup of tea be in order?

'I'm worried about my friend,' Hilda blurted out.

'Professor Silken-Grey?'

Hilda snorted.

'Never mind him. Jenny Finlay's the one. That daughter of hers tells me what's going on and I don't like it. I never liked him, that brash young man. Too young for Jenny and too old for the girl. Always round at their place. Then he went away, back to Africa or some such. Missionary work? Pah!'

Alix could only gaze, perplexed, while Hilda continued her rampage. She glared at Alix beneath lowered brows.

'You don't know who I'm talking about.'

'How can I?' Alix said with sudden spirit.

'Oliver Varley, that's who. Jenny and Saskia after the same man. They should have had more sense.'

'Is this all because of the Varley wedding?'

Hilda's colour had risen again.

'Those two next door will do Jenny down as well, the pair of them.'

'Grant and Cameron?' Alix was truly astonished. Her landlady had got some queer idea in her head about them and it was mixed up by what she was trying to say about Jenny and Saskia which made no sense either.

'I'll make us some tea,' she said, leaping into action.

'Have nothing to do with them,' Hilda said as Alix placed a mug of tea on the table at her side. 'A pair of crooks.'

'Oh no, I'm sure they're not.'

'And what do you know about them, miss? You'll do as I say if you know what's good for you.'

Alix, flushed, was not to be browbeaten.

'There is no way that I'm going to ignore Grant and Cameron.'

Hilda looked as if she would burst. Alix, concerned, put out a hand to her and then thought better of it. Home was the best place for Hilda in her present state of mind.

'I'll run you home,' she said. 'I'm planning a drive out. It's on my way.'

'If you must.' Hilda's face was paler

now and her mouth tight-lipped. She got up awkwardly, ignoring the mug of tea.

Alix resisted the temptation to offer any assistance as Hilda walked unsteadily down the path to the gate. She was thankful that she got into the car with no further show of rage.

Melting Moments

Hilda's home was even gloomier than Alix remembered with its long echoing passages. She considered contacting Jenny at once about Hilda's outburst because of the threat to her heart but then thought better of it. Alix would be seeing Jenny soon anyway when it was time to open up at the gallery.

She hadn't intended to go anywhere else in her car this morning but Hilda's pride would not have allowed her to accept the offer of a lift home if Alix had hadn't said she was going out anyway.

She turned away from the village and drove up past Nether End Farm to the top road. The next lane down took her down to a village on the Stourford road. Back then to Mellstone except that she was pulled up short by three riders on horseback who needed plenty of room to sidle by her vehicle.

Her eye was caught by something interesting in the cottage garden to her right. The *For Sale* board was for the same estate agent as the one in her own front garden, now lying face down inside the gate where it was almost hidden by nettles. This board, though, was placed in a prominent position next to a smaller wooden sign with the words *Unity Cottage* in flaking green paint.

The property was on its own in a small garden that someone had obviously tried to neaten recently by the mass of dying grass and weeds piled in one corner. Alix waited until the horses were safely past and then parked her car and got out.

Judging by the peeling paintwork on the window frames and door it was obvious that no-one loved the place but the air of neglect was somehow appealing. She wished she could buy it and love it as it should be loved.

But Hilda Lunt could.

The startling thought popped into her mind so suddenly it left her breathless. It wasn't far off the main road and other dwellings nestled nearby with neighbours for Hilda that she wouldn't admit to needing.

Being close to a bus stop was another advantage but above all the accommodation was all on one level and the garden at the back adjoined open farmland with a good view of Melbury Hill. Not visible today, of course, but there all the same.

The church and village hall promised some sort of social life if Hilda felt she needed it. Perhaps her friend, the professor, would like it? He could give village talks, why not? She would make a point of coming herself.

But what nonsense was this? Smiling at her fancies, Alix got back into the car and drove back to Mellstone. No-one could make Hilda do anything she didn't want to. She had learned that much. And who was she to advise her? Someone who refused to keep away from Cameron and his brother as ordered and would now have to take the consequences, that's who.

Time was getting on now and she was due at the gallery very soon.

But what was this on the doormat . . . a postcard? She picked it up and examined the picture of the Malvern Hills in colourful splendour before turning it over and reading Dad's bold handwriting.

'Alix, my dear, finding your own niche down there in Dorset. Pleased for you. Your old dad's doing well, too. Lois is a lovely lady and I want you to meet very soon. Considering what to do with the Kenvarloe cottage. Any ideas, like putting it on the market? Will be in touch. Love, Dad and Lois.'

Brief and to the point. Alix carried it upstairs with her and discarded her gardening clothes for jersey and skirt. Still numb with shock, she got herself to the gallery without any memory of crossing the main road or of passing the Tidings Tree.

To receive any communication from

Dad was startling but this took a great deal of thinking about. Relief first of all that he was safe. But Lois? No address on the card, of course. That was typical. And no way of getting in touch with him as he refused to carry a phone.

Alix gave herself a little shake as she crossed the empty parking area. Time enough to consider the implications of Dad's news later. But had she really found a niche for herself in the light of Hilda's ultimatum? It seemed increasingly unlikely.

To her surprise, the gallery door was locked and she needed her own keys. Usually when she got here Jenny was already in her workroom with the windows wide open to rid the place of any lingering clay smells.

She wasn't in the showroom, either. But coming across the open space outside was someone Alix recognised because she had attended the Open Day with her husband. Mrs Varley had been friendly and begged her to call them Cathy and Ralph.

'Is Jenny here?' Cathy asked breathlessly as she pushed open the showroom door and gazed round at the array of beautiful pots arranged on the shelves. 'Oh, no, I can see she isn't. But isn't this her morning for her flower rounds?'

Alix smiled.

'That's Thursday.'

'And she wouldn't be here then anyway, would she?' Her expression of dismay quickly faded to a friendly smile. 'Will she be long, do you know?'

'She'll be here any minute now. I'll make you a coffee, shall I?'

Cathy looked anxious.

'Do you have time?'

'Plenty,' Alix assured her. 'Come into the tearoom. I won't be a moment.'

She had made the coffee and produced a plate of shortbread by the time Jenny, full of apologies, came in looking so thin compared with Cathy's fuller figure that Alix was concerned.

★ ★ ★

Jenny lifted her cup to her lips and then put it down again. The migraine that had been a threat when she left home was now threatening to take over in spite of the tablets she had swallowed hastily as she left.

Cathy was full of excitement as she talked of the bridesmaids' dresses and how her daughter, Felicity, had made sure they were exactly the same shade of pink as the variety of roses she had chosen for her bouquet.

'Such a fuss,' she said. 'We never thought of such things in my day. But she's going to look really lovely and Ralph's so proud of his daughter. I am too, of course.' She paused and leaned back in her seat.

Jenny thought she saw a suggestion of tears in her friend's eyes.

'She'll be a beautiful bride,' she said gently.

Cathy let out a sigh.

'If only . . . ' She stopped, dismayed, and put her hand to her mouth.

Jenny looked down at her cup, picked

it up and began to drink. There had been awkward moments in the six years since Cathy's son, Oliver, had returned to Africa without Jenny.

But during his brief visits home there had been no hard feelings between the two so why did Cathy assume it would be difficult now when he returned for his sister's wedding?

'It will be a busy time for you in June with family here for the wedding,' she said. Oliver hadn't been home for quite a while but of course he would come and bring the rest of the family, too.

'They're coming before the wedding,' Cathy said almost, it seemed, in apology. 'Quite soon, in fact, on a Song leave.'

'That will be nice for you.'

'And for Ralph.' Cathy's face clouded. 'They're so lucky having their twins, such dear little girls. Faith wanted to have a large family but it's not to be. But they're content.'

Jenny nodded. She had been content with Saskia, too, although there was always a deep-down sadness that there were to be no more babies. But all that was so long ago and she had struggled to make a life for them both after the break-up of her marriage.

Cathy finished her coffee and placed the cup in her saucer with a clatter. She hesitated for a moment.

'They're talking of coming home for good and want to look for somewhere to live in this area. Ralph's over the moon.'

'I'm sure he is.' A good thing, too, Jenny thought, even if his desire for a son and grandson to follow him on the family farm had been thwarted. She made an attempt to smile.

'Tell me about the girls. I don't even know their names. They're coming up for three, aren't they?'

'Rosie and Eva.' In her eagerness to comply, Cathy leaned forward and was prevented from knocking her cup off the table by some quick action from Jenny.

By the time Cathy stood up to go,

Jenny felt her head reeling. No work-room for her today, she thought. In fact her migraine was so bad it would be good to lie down on her bed in a dark-ened room and let the world go on without her.

The kitchen at Marigold Cottage was a mess when she got there. Jenny looked round in disbelief at the clutter of pans and utensils in the sink and the array of cooking paraphernalia covering all the worktops and the table too. Saskia her-self was covered in a layer of flour.

'The bag broke,' she said in answer to Jenny's obvious consternation.

'But what do you think you're doing?'

Saskia was sulky.

'What does it look like?'

'Get it cleared up at once. You're needed at the gallery. Alix is on her own.'

Saskia glared.

'But I'm going out. Michelle will be here in a minute. We're going to make plans.'

'Put her off.'

'Why should I?'

'Just do it!'

Jenny seldom lost her temper these days and as she lay on her bed upstairs and heard the crashing down below she felt shame overtake her. Saskia was doing her best but it wasn't enough. She needed responsibility, something to make her feel her own worth and she wasn't getting it.

She heard a crash from the front door and then silence.

*　*　*

Alix had expected Saskia sooner and was grateful that it was still early and no customers had yet appeared.

She was in the tearoom checking the freshness of the flowers on the tables when there was the sound of rushing footsteps. Moments later Saskia burst in, flushed of face and breathing hard.

She thrust a huge cake tin towards Alix.

'I made these.' She flopped down on

137

the nearest chair and ran a hand over her forehead. 'Mum's in a strop. Really angry. I couldn't bear it.'

Alix thought of Jenny's pale face but wisely made no comment. She took the tin and opened it. Inside were layers of delicious-looking biscuits with red showing through the layers of white caster sugar.

'Raspberry jam?' she asked.

Saskia nodded.

'Melting moments, they're called. I thought they'd do for here.'

Alix was pleased.

'Do? They'll more than do. Can I sample one now?'

'To check they're good enough?'

'How critical do you think I am?'

'Pretty bad,' Saskia said and grinned. Alix smiled, too.

'Bring them through to the kitchen.'

'Tidy,' Saskia commented, looking round. 'I wish I knew how you did it. I left the one at home in a bit of a mess.'

Alix took a bite from her melting moment.

'They're well-named,' she said. 'It melted in my mouth. Can I have another?'

'Why not? They're yours.'

'Mine?'

'For the tearoom,' Saskia said in exasperated tones. 'I thought people might like them.'

'How did you make them, Saskia? They're magnificent.'

Saskia flushed.

'You like them?' She sounded as if she really wanted to know.

Alix felt her heart warm. This was the closeness between them that Jenny hoped for and believed they had already achieved.

Saskia swept imaginary dust off the worktop, looked at her fingers and sighed.

'A family recipe, deadly secret.'

'Oh.' Alix took a step back. But Saskia smiled.

'I just threw things together. You'll need to know the exact amounts. Ask Gran. She'll tell you. Give her a buzz and see what she says.'

'Oh, I couldn't. I hardly know her.'

139

Elisabeth Ellis, Jenny's mother, had been friendly at the Open Day but she could hardly demand family recipes from her just like that.

'Then I will,' Saskia said. She whipped out her phone and seconds later it was done. 'You're invited to tea at Nether End on Tuesday. Gran says it's a good opportunity to get to know you properly.'

'But you know I can't go.'

'Of course you can. Mum'll only be off today. She's never ill. And I'll cope here. You can't back out now.'

And it seemed Alix couldn't. She didn't want to, either. Here was the chance to create a happier atmosphere between them at last. She hoped it would always be like this.

By lunchtime there were sounds outside. The delivery of the paving stones? It seemed so from the racket going on as they were unloaded from the lorry that had backed itself in the car park.

The workmen arrived in the afternoon and with them came Cameron.

Her heart lifted to see him and she felt a flush in her cheeks as she greeted him. A brief smile from him, that was all, and he was off to deal with the matter in hand. Well, what did she expect?

She made coffee for two men working at laying the paving stones outside and put some of the melting moments on a plate for the young man and woman who arrived in the tearoom at that moment.

She and Cameron drank their coffee in the kitchen.

'They don't want me breathing down their necks,' Cameron said as he sat down with his back to the patio doors.

She could smell his aftershave now that they were seated close to each other and felt a disturbing dull ache in the pit of her stomach. But she must make an effort, concentrate on something else. A quick look outside to check progress and she felt calmer.

'You made a good choice with these paving stones,' she said.

'Did I?'

'They make the place seem bigger.'

'I'll grant you that.' He put out his hand to take one of melting moments from the tin she held towards him and took a bite.

'Delicious. May I?' He took another.

★　★　★

'Homemade, I take it?'

'Made by Saskia. Melting moments, she calls them.'

'Aha! A peace offering?'

'I'd like to think so.'

'Mellstone Moments is a good name.'

'Mellstone Moments? Brilliant!' Alix smiled, delighted. 'People seem to like them. The couple who came in just before you said how different they were. They're going to come back again with friends.

'It's odd, don't you think, that we could be well known for something so simple?' She had wanted a signature

dish and melting moments made by
Saskia and named by Cameron could
well be that.

Cameron leaned forward to replace
the lid on the tin.

'Don't tempt me further or there'll
be none left.'

Alix should have felt relieved that they
had discovered something that was good
but now she thought that something
was not quite right. Saskia's Moments,
she thought. Not Alix's. What would
Olaf think? Now there was a question.

She stared into space, startled when
Cameron spoke again.

'I'll be off, then,' he said, standing
up. 'Thanks for the coffee and Mellstone Moments.'

'I'll have to go away from here,' she
said.

Cameron looked horrified.

'You're not serious?'

'About what?'

'Alix, what's wrong?'

She gazed at him blankly.

'Wrong?'

'You're not making sense.'

Of course she was. She needed to work Dad's bombshell out, that was all. She couldn't ask Olaf about anything because he wasn't here and in any case it wasn't the sort of thing he would have even have considered because his mind would have been on other, higher things. Like . . . what?

She shook her head and got up.

'Sorry, I was thinking. I meant that I need to go down to Cornwall for a few days sometime soon.'

He looked relieved.

'If that's all it was?'

She smiled.

'I'm all right, Cameron. Don't worry.'

'I'll try not to.'

He gave a backward glance as he returned to the patio but then shrugged and moved on.

She watched him go, a dedicated man, a perfectionist, someone you could rely on. Easy then, for her to avoid him.

Surprise Discovery

Alix set off on Tuesday evening to visit Nether End Farm. She had passed it often enough on her rambles and had liked the way it fitted so perfectly in its surroundings of wide green lawns backed by the wooded hillside. There must be farm buildings, too, but they were out of sight.

Even though the sky was a mass of grey with darker clouds looming over the downs Alix felt her spirits rising. She had decided to walk in spite of the threat of rain and was glad she had when the scent of new-mown grass greeted her as she walked down the drive to the house.

She heard, in the distance, the faintest murmur of woodpigeons. A tractor, too, now, vying with them but not quite winning. Alix was still smiling when the door opened and she was ushered into the wide hall that smelled of furniture polish and lavender.

Elisabeth Ellis, Saskia's grandmother, looked as elegant as she had at the Open Day and her smile was as warm.

'It's good to see you again, Alix,' she said as they went into the long sitting-room at the back of the house. 'Saskia was telling us how well the tearoom is doing. Jenny must be pleased.' A slightly worried look flashed across her face and was gone. 'And you're happy there?'

'Oh, yes, very.'

Elisabeth indicated the low comfortable chairs near the French windows.

'Please, sit down. My husband will bring in the tea shortly.'

Beneath her feet the patterned carpet in faded shades of blues and mauves was so right for the old-fashioned room that Alix gave a sigh of pleasure. Requesting a cake recipe here seemed out of place but there was no need for her to raise the subject because Elisabeth did so herself in such a kind way that Alix felt welcome here in a way she hadn't expected.

Elisabeth removed an exercise book from the bottom drawer of the bureau in the corner.

'I remember making these years ago when Saskia was a little girl.' She was silent for a moment, her head bent over the notebook in her lap. Alix, looking at her, was reminded of her friend and boss back there in Cornwall, who had arranged for her own presence here in Mellstone. Two sympathetic women.

There was the sound of activity now and John Ellis, handsome in tweeds and checked shirt, came in, stooping slightly over a laden trolley. He straightened to his full height, smiling with pleasure at seeing Alix.

'No, don't get up, my dear,' he said.

'Alix, this is John, my husband and Jenny's stepfather.' Her voice softened a little. 'John, this is Alix who is doing, such good work in setting up the tearoom at the gallery.'

His smile was warm as he bowed slightly.

'We've been hearing such excellent

things about you, Alix.'

Alix smiled, too. He seemed a kind man. Jenny had told her how his family had farmed at Nether End for generations but now he relied solely on his manager to continue the business, having no sons to follow him.

He looked at his wife, who returned his loving look.

'John's in the middle of something in the study,' Elisabeth said in explanation as he withdrew.

They talked a little of how well the tearoom was doing, especially after the introduction of the Mellstone Moments.

'Saskia made some more yesterday,' Alix said.

Elisabeth looked anxious.

'At Marigold Cottage?'

'In the tearoom kitchen.'

'I hope she didn't leave it in a mess?'

'Well, no.'

'She's improved then. You should be thankful.'

★ ★ ★

Alix had much to think about on her return to the village. The Ellises' happiness was plain to see. Wonderful, in fact. So why shouldn't the same be true for Dad and Lois? She hoped he, too, had found happiness.

But all those years he had been on his own there had never been any hint that he wanted a change and now in a matter of weeks he was in a relationship that would change his life. Lois? Alix wished she knew more about her. Not for the first time she wished Dad carried a phone.

The hedges were the same now as they had been when she had come this way earlier but somehow they had lost their brilliance.

The birds were silent and there was no sound of the distant tractor.

But it was useless to conjecture and to worry about the likely sale of the cottage down in Cornwall.

Alix had chosen to come away from

there but the thought of it was always in the back of her mind as something permanent. But how selfish to consider herself at a time like this!

She was passing Trevose Lodge, Hilda Lunt's rambling home, just as Jenny came out of the gate and latched it behind her.

Jenny smiled to see her but Alix could see that it wasn't with any true warmth. She looked pale, too, with dark shadows beneath her eyes.

'Hilda's well, I hope,' Alix said as she slowed down a little as Jenny fell in step beside her.

'As bossy as usual, I'm afraid. She thinks I'm working too hard and should take a rest. I do feel rather a wreck, I suppose. There's a lot to think about.'

'Saskia's Mellstone Moments are really taking off in the tearoom,' Alix said.

Jenny nodded as if she hadn't really heard but Alix continued to talk in an optimistic way about her visit to Nether End farm in the hope that she would do some good.

'The rounds I do on Thursday sorting out the flowers and so on at the businesses on my rota is beginning to seem like a waste of time,' Jenny said as they reached the main road and the parting of their ways.

'I sometimes fear that it's the same with all of it. But take no notice of me, Alix, it's a pleasure to have you here, believe me.'

Her smile as they separated was a little brighter but Alix continued along the lane to Meadowlands with a heavy heart. She was beginning to fear that the same thing might apply to herself.

*   *   *

Alix's phone chirruped as she sat down to breakfast next morning. She reached across to pick it up. Jenny! To Alix's dismay her voice sounded weak as if were almost too much of an effort to speak.

'I'm taking Hilda's advice,' Jenny said. 'I've an appointment at the doctor's this morning so I'll be late in.'

This was a surprise. Jenny hadn't looked her normal self when they had met outside Trevose Lodge yesterday evening but there certainly hadn't been any mention of advice from Hilda. This was worrying.

Alix kept her voice light.

'No need to worry about anything, Jenny. I'll get there early and open up. Thank you for letting me know.'

'He's fitting me in before surgery. He's an old friend. I shouldn't be too late.'

'I'll see you later, then.' Alix clicked off her phone.

Deep in thought, she finished her toast and marmalade. There had been no mention of any help from Saskia. It seemed she would be on her own for the time Jenny was away but that was all right because it was unusual to have many prospective customers until nearly coffee time and by then Jenny might be back.

But as the morning wore on Alix began to feel edgy. Several people were in for coffee, the same elderly couple that made a habit of calling in most days and group of six friends from Hilbury who were interested in visiting the showroom and disappointed that Jenny wasn't here this time but they would come again.

'I'm expecting her very soon,' Alix told them. 'In fact, I'll try her mobile and see what's happening. She's probably been held up.'

It was answered at once, by Saskia in a tone of voice that sounded exasperated.

'Mum wants to speak to you. Here she is.'

'I'm home now, Alix, but there's been a bit of bother. It was the shock of the doctor ordering me to take a week's rest that made me stumble on the surgery step and injure my ankle. My blood pressure shot up even higher when I found myself in Accident and Emergency.'

Alix was horrified.

'You've broken your ankle?'

'A bad sprain. I have to keep it up.

How's business? Saskia will be with you at lunchtime and for the afternoon so if you're not too busy could you leave her to it and call in here?'

'Of course I will.'

★　★　★

Jenny, lying on her sofa in Marigold Cottage with her injured foot high up on one arm of it, looked relieved to see Alix.

'Come and sit near me and tell me how things have been going today.'

Alix smiled.

'Very few people in today which is just as well. Saskia's made a start on dusting some of the shelves and being very careful about putting everything back as it was. I've made some more ginger biscuits and all the tins are now full.'

'That's good. I expect the table decorations need changing, though?'

'I was going to ask you about that.'

'There are plenty of flowers here in the garden. Could you pick some and do that for me? Take what you need and use the oasis that's already in the pots. You've used oasis before?'

'Well, no.' This was going to be a steep learning curve.

'Make sure it's wet. It's what we use for flower arranging. You just stick the stems in and they stay where you want them.'

'I see.' It sounded easy enough but she must seem a complete idiot, sitting here looking perplexed. But Jenny smiled kindly at her.

'You can do it, Alix, I'm sure. Call in again on your way home and tell me how you got on.'

The back garden at Marigold Cottage was reached by climbing up a flight of stone steps. Alix was interested to see that in a sheltered spot by the far wall the hanging flower buds of the wisteria were showing purple.

But she was here to pick a few suitable flowers for the tearoom tables. Some bright pinks in the bed at the corner caught her eye. Small dwarf ones, yes . . . just the thing. She then gave her attention to some shiny green leaves nearby that would set them off to perfection in the colourful pots placed ready for them.

She carried her spoils back to the gallery kitchen and spent much longer than she felt she should on arranging the pinks to her satisfaction. She placed them on the tables and stood back see the effect.

'Not bad,' Saskia said grudgingly. 'I'd hardly know where to start.'

Jenny had already told Alix that Saskia was hopeless with flowers. A sudden thought struck Alix. Tomorrow was Jenny's flower-rota day.

'I have to ask you a huge favour,' Jenny said later, looking anxious. 'Would you be prepared to take over the flower arranging for me tomorrow?'

Alix, horrified, thought of Jenny's expertise with flowers and her own lack of knowledge.

'But how can I possibly manage?'

'There's no-one else I can ask. You're

calm and reliable and don't fuss. And you're good with colour, Alix. I'm confident you'll sort them out in the various containers to good advantage. And don't worry about it. Cathy Varley will come in and keep Saskia company while you're away so you can take your time.'

Reluctantly, Alix agreed. She had no choice but to do the best she could but she wasn't happy.

The flowers needed were on order at the florists in Hilbury to be picked up soon after the place opened. Five venues on the rota, miles apart in some cases. No more hints or questions but it couldn't be as simple as Jenny made out, Alix thought. She would find out tomorrow.

Hilbury early on a Thursday morning was busier than Alix expected. Delivery vans were blocking the narrow street so that she had to wait for quite a while before she could get to the other side.

As she stepped on to the pavement she recognised someone emerging from the estate agent's, in one hand was a sheet of paper that looked like house details and in the other a knobbly walking stick. This was Professor Silken-Grey, wearing emerald trousers and with his greying hair tied back so tightly it looked as if the roots were being wrenched out of his forehead.

She smiled.

His blue eyes glinted at her.

'Have we met before?'

'At your lecture the other evening.' He bowed slightly.

'I think you must be house-hunting, too?'

Alix didn't know what gave him that idea.

'No. I . . . '

'I trust that you're not doing so on someone's behalf who is as stubborn as my sister.'

'Your sister?'

He glared down at the paper in his hand.

'Here's a perfect place for the two of us. But will she hear of it? Oh, no. But that's Hilda all over. As stubborn as they come.'

'Miss Lunt is your sister?' Alix said.

'I assume you know her well?'

'She's my landlady.'

He nodded.

'Ah.' A wealth of meaning in the word. 'She has spoken of you. Allow me to talk of this further. I'd like to commission your help.' He pointed his stick at the building next door. This was a coffee shop that looked from the outside a rough sort of place with a high wooden bench across the width of it.

Seated on one of the high stools a few minutes later with her feet on the rung, Alix thought of how bizarre this was. The professor had manoeuvred her in here so easily that dealing with Hilda Lunt would surely be a doddle for him and she wondered that he needed her input.

Their coffee came in tall earthenware mugs. He stared at his as if he wondered how it got there.

'Hilda needs something smaller than that great place falling down round her ears,' he said. 'Important structural damage will have to be dealt with. I

159

know full well it would put off any prospective purchaser except someone completely out of his mind.

'But that's not the issue. She knows that we should buy a place together but will she consider it? Oh, no, not my pig-headed sister. Look at this.' He spread out the paper in front of her.

Interested, Alix looked.

'Unity Cottage!'

'You know it?'

'I've seen it from the outside.'

His expression brightened.

'May I have your opinion?'

'I liked the look of it.'

'It needs work done, of course, but that wouldn't matter. I'd be grateful to be living there and so would my sister if she allowed herself to borrow money. It could be possible with a bit of negotiating. We'd need to move quickly.'

'But can't she . . . ?'

'Put her place on the market at once as it is? The proceeds from her sale of that place will be very little. I'm under no illusions.'

He picked up the page of house details, folded it and put it in his pocket.

'I have an appointment to view this morning. A waste of time, I fear.'

There seemed to be nothing to say to this. He looked so downcast she wished she could help but couldn't imagine how.

'You'll talk to her, make her see reason?'

'But I can't!'

'You can't?' He looked depressed.

'I mean it's not possible. I've refused to do something she wanted and she went off, furious with me. I'm the last person you should ask.'

He looked surprised.

'She ordered you to do something and you refused?'

'I'm sorry.'

'She made no mention of it. She was pleased with the way you look after the cottage, that's all. I assure you that's the truth.'

'I see.' It proved nothing even if it

were true. 'But why would she listen to me anyway?'

He made no answer to that but got to his feet and bowed with courtesy. Only afterwards as she went into the damp and sweet-smelling atmosphere of the florist's did it occur to her that he might think that someone who refused to do something on her orders might incur Hilda's respect.

Fat chance of that!

Unlikely Assistant

Alix had known that Jenny's large order of flowers would be ready for her to collect but not that there would be so many containers of them. She saw delphiniums, lupins and multi-coloured alstroemerias amongst them and some she didn't recognise.

The assistant, a motherly woman with a purple apron tied loosely around her waist, closed each cardboard container with care.

She beamed at Alix.

'I've marked each of the boxes with their contents to make it easier for you. That's what Jenny suggested.'

'Thank you.'

'She's well, I hope? Tell her Maisie was asking after her. Now, dear, I'll help you outside with them. Is your car outside?'

Alix piled the boxes into her car. A farewell wave to Maisie in the doorway and she was off. On the outskirts of town, she was followed by a vehicle that appeared not to want to overtake. A large one, a Land Rover. Cameron's Land Rover? Her heart jolted in surprise.

She pulled in as soon as she could and wound down her window as he came to join her. He was wearing a grey jacket, unzipped, with a royal-blue shirt beneath unbuttoned at the neck.

'You've forgotten something,' he said. 'One of your containers. That poor woman looked shocked as I swept it up off the pavement and set off. She's probably phoning the police at this very moment and I'll be picked up at the next check-point.'

Alix gave a gurgle of laughter.

'And what do you expect to happen after that?'

He grinned.

'Who knows? Slung into jail? Deported?'

His words had given her the chance to recover but her hands were still shaking a little. She had thought Cameron was miles away visiting some outpost of the UK before leaving this area for good. She opened her car door and got out too.

'Won't you tell me which one it is it is?'

'You mean you have no idea?' He led his head a little to one side and the corners of his mouth twitched.

She swung round to look at her car as if she had x-ray eyes.

'I don't know.' She hated to admit it but it was true. Anyone with any sense would have counted the containers in the shop and again when they were loaded. What sort of fool would she have looked if she had turned up minus fresh flowers at the last place on her rounds?

'I was thinking,' she said, 'about Professor Silken-Grey's sister.'

'The chap who gave the talk?'

'That one.'

'Why his sister? You know her, then?'

'You do, too. Hilda Lunt.' Now she had surprised him. 'He was doing a bit of house-hunting. He wants me to persuade her to move out of her place and for

165

them to buy something together.'

'Miles from here, I hope,' Cameron said with feeling.

'He's afraid that it's unlikely to be anywhere. Her place won't fetch much because of the massive amount of work needed on it.'

He whistled.

'I see. Poor man.'

'She simply won't consider it anyway.'

'That follows. Independent to the last, our Hilda. Well, good luck with the persuading, Alix. It won't do you much good, though, if she sees you here with me. This is the main road from Hilbury to Mellstone, don't forget. She's sure to pop up somewhere. Quick, let's get off it. Where are you going with all those boxes?'

'Winthrop Major. The Manor Hotel. I'm standing in for Jenny as a flower arranger.'

He showed no surprise.

'Right then. Let's get going. I'll follow you.'

Bemused as she was from the unexpected sight of him, she got back into her car and concentrated hard on driving down narrow twisting lanes to find the hotel. Maisie in the florist's had told her it was the main street of the village and couldn't be missed. And so it proved.

Cameron followed her into the car park and got out of his vehicle to accompany her into the vestibule of the hotel.

'You don't have to do this,' she said.

'But you'd like my moral support?'

'It's the first time I've done anything like it.' She spoke hurriedly because coming towards them, smiling, was a slim young man wearing a very smart suit.

'Adam Smallbone, manager,' he said with a smile. 'Miss Finlay has just telephoned to explain the situation. I believe you are her assistant?'

'That's right.' Alix shook his outstretched hand. 'Alix Williams. And this is . . .'

'Cameron Sutherland,' Cameron said swiftly, 'here to help too.'

'Then come this way. I'll show you what needs doing.'

'The assistant's assistant,' Cameron

167

murmured as they followed him up a broad staircase to the first landing.

It turned out that Jenny had been contracted for five arrangements at the Manor Hotel, all of them in large ceramic containers of her own design already in place. Jenny had told her that these were to be attended to where they were and that was a relief. The others in the hall and reception rooms on the ground floor were even larger.

'I hardly know where to begin,' Alix said when she and Cameron were out in the open air again.

He smiled.

'Let's take a look those boxes of flowers first.'

'Good advice.'

He helped lift them out and the one he had rescued joined them on the ground.

'One arrangement at a time, I think.' He made a rapid selection from the containers of red iris and multi-coloured alstroemerias.

Another box contained greenery and

168

sprigs of yellow mimosa. His expertise surprised her and yet it shouldn't have done. He was a botanist, after all, and she was content to leave the selection of flowers to him.

When it was finished it looked magnificent. In all the colours of fire, it lit up the landing in a spectacular way.

By the time they had done the last of the arrangements in the largest of the reception rooms a group of interested guests was watching them. Alix made sure that she placed some of Jenny's business cards nearby.

Cameron paused when they reached the cars.

'You did well. You should be proud of yourself.'

Alix opened her boot and he lifted the emptied containers in for her.

'Hardly. All I did was pass the appropriate flowers to you. I'm the assistant here.'

'And a fast-learning one.'

She laughed, as she checked the list

Jenny had given her and then was serious again.

'The next two places are for table decorations and desks in the reception areas. Jenny said it's easier this time as there's a room set aside for the work.'

'So she threw you in at the deep end with this one?'

Alix was immediately on the defensive.

'It's the way the route pans out.'

'So where next? We should be on our way.'

She turned to face him.

'Thank you, Cameron. I think I can manage now. You've been a tremendous help but now I must do the rest on my own.' She smiled.

'But why? I'd like to help you, Alix.'

She tried to remonstrate but he waved one hand as if brushing her words aside. So much for keeping her distance from him! She thrust her shoulders back. It would be so easy to accept, to stand back at each place and listen to his excellent advice. But Jenny had confidence in her. She must have confidence in herself.

His hand was already on the door of his car.

'Now, where is the next place on the list?'

She shrugged. She wasn't going to tell him but how was she going to convince him she was in earnest? She took a deep breath.

'I'm staying right here until you drive off, Cameron. I mean it.'

His eyes narrowed and for a moment he seemed undecided about what to do, then he smiled.

'I believe you do. You're as bad as our Hilda, not knowing what's good for you. Well, so be it.'

She watched him go, forcing herself not to betray by the slightest movement what her insistence had cost her. But she needed this. For too long had she relied on others when she should have taken time to consider things for herself. Like her job offer in Mellstone, for instance, and the offer of the cottage that came at just the right moment. All so easy when she came to think about it. Too easy.

At the next place, a small guesthouse on the outskirts of Stourford, she was greeted by a flustered receptionist and left to her own devices in the flower room at the back of the property.

One of the flower boxes, the one she had carelessly left on the pavement, had a label announcing that the contents were for posies. Just the thing for here. She found bunches of violets and small pieces of grape hyacinths amongst others of a suitable small size for Jenny's pretty pots. Because she had done something similar arranging the table decorations in the tearoom this was enjoyable.

At the next place a sandwich lunch was provided. After that, the afternoon sped by.

Alix remembered Jenny's tip about using the same fresh flowers to replace the dead ones in the oasis which worked well and made her task so much easier. Her confidence was growing with each one.

All the time her hands were busy arranging the flowers at the last place on the rota, Alix's mind was hard at work, too. Cameron had likened her to Hilda Lunt in her insistence that she didn't know what was good for her and that had hurt.

Hadn't she proved to herself by coming to Mellstone that her decision was the right one? Might not Hilda feel that she knew what was best for her too and be equally right? But no. Hilda's stubbornness was unreasonable. Because of it, her brother might lose the chance of purchasing Unity Cottage and their moving in. together.

By refusing Cameron's generous offer of assistance she, on the other hand, was merely showing Jenny and ultimately herself, that she was capable of doing something required of her. Cameron must surely understand that?

So why this deadly ache of regret when she had watched him fumble with his car keys before driving off?

★　★　★

Back in Mellstone Alix found that the tearoom was still busy. Saskia, in a frilly white apron, greeted her with shining eyes as she came into the kitchen. Obviously, her day had gone well.

'There's someone here who wants to book in a walking group for lunch tomorrow. Good idea or what?'

'Oh, definitely good if they're happy with soup and rolls.'

'Cheese rolls — with Dorset's Blue Vinny cheese, of course, and salad. I told them we could do that.'

Alix nodded.

'Easy enough if they'll be satisfied. Shall I have a word?'

Saskia indicated an elderly woman seated on her own at the table in the window.

'No, don't get up, please,' Alix said as she approached, 'I hear you'd like to make a booking?'

The enthusiasm was heart-warming.

'I'm Pam Digby of the Shenston Scramblers. I love it here in Mellstone and it's a good halfway point for our

174

Friday walk. The lunch menu sounds just right for us, too. Nice and light. And can we have plenty of those delicious local cakey-biscuity things? Best thing I've tasted in ages.'

Alix smiled, aware of Saskia's pleasure.

'Mellstone Moments? Of course. The soup for tomorrow is butternut squash and ginger and there'll be another choice as well.'

'Perfect. My mouth's watering. And I'd like to take some of your cards to pass round the group. I believe those charming little flower vases are for sale too?'

'You like them? There's a shelf of them on display in the showroom.'

'Thank you, my dear. And there's one other thing.' She paused. 'I hardly like to ask but is it possible to park our cars here while we do the walk? From about ten o'clock? Four cars, I think. Or maybe five.'

'That won't be a problem.'

'And neither will it be,' Alix said to

Saskia when Pam Digby had gone and she was locking the outside door. 'It will be a good advertisement for us. It will show we're a popular place. I hope you have a good supply of Mellstone Moments in the cake tins ready for the onslaught?'

'I wish. I could make some more but not at home. Mum would go mad.'

They were back in the kitchen now. Saskia had made a start on the clearing up but there was still some to do and it was up to Alix to do it. Tiredness came over her so suddenly she flopped down on a chair at the table.

'You could do the baking at my place,' she said. The words had slipped out but it wasn't a bad idea.

'This evening, you mean?'

'Why not? I can make myself scarce and leave you to it. There's someone I should see.' She got to her feet. 'I'll finish here now so off you go. You've done a good job here, Saskia. Thank you.'

Only later, as she washed up the dish

she had used for her simple meal at Meadowlands, did Alix realise that she had sounded supremely confident and in charge when talking to Saskia.

Maybe it was because she was aware she had done a reasonable day's work herself. She dried her hands, smiling. Now that she was rested she might consider calling on her landlady to enquire how she was and even, she took a deep breath, put in a good word for Unity Cottage.

Her mobile rang.

'Dad? Where are you?' she asked.

'Lois wanted to stay here in Malvern a while longer. We'll be heading south tomorrow, making for Kenvarloe. But never mind that.

'We've got important things to discuss about the cottage now that the tenants have moved out. We need to get it cleared out for a start. And Lois wants to meet you. How are you fixed for taking a couple of days off and joining us there? Soon if you can. I'm having to consider the future of the place, as I said.'

'The future?'

'That's why we need to talk.' She was horrified.

'You wouldn't put our home on the market?'

'Not without your consent, Alix.'

'But Olaf's belongings are there.' This was like an act of betrayal and the suddenness of his request almost took her breath away.

'And I can't come now, Dad. It's not possible until Jenny's back at work. She's injured and I'm in charge. I can't let her down.' Her disappointment was acute. 'I'm happy for you and I want to meet Lois.' She took a deep breath. That much was true. 'Please, Dad, leave some things to me, Olaf's things.' Her voice broke and she had to pause to regain her composure.

'Ah, Olaf,' he said.

They had hardly talked of Olaf since the day of his funeral.

'Alix, are you still there?' A worried note had entered her father's voice.

'I'm . . . yes, I'm here.'

Dad was giving her the chance to be there with him when the place was cleared but it was too sudden. It meant reliving memories of Olaf and she wasn't ready for that.

A Heavy Heart

Alix had some thinking to do. After her father's startling revelation, Meadowlands felt claustrophobic. Saskia would be here soon, prepared for an evening of baking. And chat, probably. No way. The baking, yes. That was essential for the good of the business but not the discussion of everyday things that seemed to have no relevance to what she was facing now.

She snatched a pair of scissors from the kitchen drawer and went out into the front garden just as Saskia arrived, laden with a bag bulging with the vital ingredients for her Mellstone Moments.

'Hi, I'm here.'

She looked radiant and Alix, beside her, felt awkward and unattractive.

'I was just going out.'

Saskia glanced at the scissors in her hand.

'With those?'

'I have to pick some flowers first.'

'And then what?'

'They're for Hilda Lunt.' Now where had that come from? Alix was as surprised as Saskia appeared to be.

'What's that a reward for, then?'

All at once Alix knew. Not a reward but in answer to a request by a man wanting to do the best for his sister.

From the abundance of flowers in the front garden, half-hidden by strangling undergrowth, Hilda must have loved them once. This had been her childhood home and the professor's too, now she came to think of it.

Alix smiled.

'A gesture of sympathy, that's all.'

'And the best of luck. I can get on then, can I?'

'Lock up when you go. I don't know how long I'll be.'

'Five minutes, I expect.'

Alix left her scissors by the front gate and set off along the lane with her bunch of forget-me-knots and lilies-of-the-valley.

This was an impulsive act but the feel of cold stems in her hand was comforting.

'Come in, why don't you?' Hilda's deep voice ordered as soon as she rang the doorbell.

She should be used to this, Alix thought, as she went into the dim room at the end of the passage. Hilda was sitting in a deep armchair by the window with her leg propped up awkwardly on a low stool.

'I expected my brother,' she said.

Alix held out the flowers to her.

'I've brought you these, Miss Lunt, from your garden.'

Hilda took them from her in silence and for a dreadful moment Alix expected her to throw them back at her. Instead Hilda stared at them, frowning, and then bent to hold them close to her face. The scent from the lilies-of-of-the-valley was stronger now. A clock ticked from the sideboard. Somewhere outside a bird twittered and then was silent.

'Not from my garden here,' Hilda said at last. 'It's a wilderness out there and no-one cares.'

'Your brother cares.'

'Only for himself.'

'I don't think that's true.'

'And what do you know about it, miss? You hardly know him.'

Alix wasn't going to argue. She had been asked to make Hilda change her mind about moving into a more suitable place but it would be a thankless task.

'They're from the Meadowlands' front garden,' she said. 'I thought you'd like them.'

The front garden of the Cornish cottage was a wilderness too but there were no flowers blooming beneath the mass of weeds. Alix thought of Dad and Lois who meant so much to each other. She hung her head and stared at the dusty carpet.

'So what's the matter with you?' Hilda's words sounded abrupt but there was something softer in her tone now.

Alix took an unsteady breath. She had never told anyone what Olaf had meant to her, only hinted a little of it to Cameron.

Now she told of their life together right from the early years and how Flotsam Follies had flourished and been popular with the tourists.

She could almost smell the salty sea breeze on her face as she dwelt on the beachcombing expeditions she and Olaf had enjoyed together, especially in the winter months when raging seas had rendered a rich harvest on the beaches. Her hands clenched in her lap as she told of the horror of Olaf's death.

'Olaf wanted me to go with him that day,' Alix whispered. 'I might have stopped him leaning too far over the cliff. He might still be alive.'

The silence felt oppressive, bending down on her in a huge weight.

'Would he have listened to you?' Hilda said at last.

Alix shook her head.

'I don't know.' And yet she did know, had always known that when Olaf had an idea in his head all his energies were focused on it and he was oblivious to anything else. That was his strength and she had admired him for it.

'Cameron criticised him and I couldn't bear it and now he's going away and I can't bear that, either.'

Alix's voice shuddered to a stop. She had said too much — and to Hilda of all people! Ashamed, she got unsteadily to her feet.

Afterwards she wondered that Hilda had said nothing else but had sat quite still gazing down at the flowers in her lap. But what was there to say when someone blurted out something like that?

★ ★ ★

She seemed destined to walk about the lanes in a dazed state, Alix thought as she arrived outside Meadowlands. Still shocked at the way her deepest anxieties had come pouring out, her first thought had been to walk up the track to the top of the downs where no-one would see her. But already the sky was dimming into dusk.

To see the blurry figure of Cameron standing by his gate brandishing a pair of scissors surprised her.

He held them out to her.

'Yours? I've just found them. How come you dropped them without noticing?'

She took them from him.

'I was cutting some flowers.' He raised his eyebrows.

'More of them? Surely not.'

'For Miss Lunt.'

'That's a surprise.'

Her face flamed.

'Why should it matter that I've picked a bunch of flowers from her own garden to give to her? She was kind to me.' Her breath caught in her throat. 'I told her things, important things, and she listened.'

'And did you persuade her to do what her brother wants?'

Alix started to speak and then was pulled up short. What sort of emissary was she to come away without at least trying to do what she had been asked?

She shook her head.

Cameron looked at her intently.

'Please, Alix, go and get some rest. It would have been a waste of time anyway.' He smiled briefly and was gone.

She listened to his footsteps as he walked up the garden path next door as if it were the last time she would hear them. Perhaps it was. She had lashed out at him for no good reason and was ashamed.

With a heavy heart she went indoors.

Moments later there was tapping at the back door. She flew to open it. The light from behind her fell full on Cameron's familiar face. For a moment she couldn't speak and neither, it seemed, could he.

'Cameron?' she said at last.

He cleared his throat.

'I was supposed to give you this.'

He held out an envelope. She took it gingerly.

'It won't bite,' he said. 'It's an invitation. From Grant. You'll see. I hope you can come?'

'I'd better open it.'

'Later will do. Alix?'

'Yes?'

'I'm leaving on Saturday. I wanted you to know.'

There was something in his glance that made her throat dry. She swallowed.

'I thought you'd leave without telling me.'

'Do you think as little of me as that?'

She realised suddenly that she should have invited him in but now it seemed too late because he turned to go as if he felt he'd said too much. Too much or too little? It was all the same really. Confused, she stood at the open doorway until she could hear his footsteps no longer. Was she always to hear his footsteps fading away?

She closed the door.

A Reassuring Promise

On the kitchen table was a plate of Mellstone Moments with a note.

'Thanks for the use of your amenities — such as they are! I'd thought you'd like to sample some of the results. Don't eat them all at once! See you tomorrow. I'll be there at lunchtime to help out. Love, Saskia x'

Tears sprang to Alix's eyes. This thoughtfulness was something she hadn't bargained for. Offhand, sulky, seeming not to care about anyone but herself, that was Saskia. Until now. Was it too much to hope that it would last?

A large soothing cup of hot chocolate was needed here. She lingered over making it and then sat down at the table with the chocolatey steam rising in front of her and Dulled out the envelope Cameron had given her.

An invitation. On blue card. Grant

was giving a farewell party at home for his brother on Thursday evening and hoped she would come. Just a few friends and neighbours, nothing formal.

She sat and looked at it, remembering the last time there had been an invitation from next door. It had been a barbecue in Grant's beautiful garden with Grant, in white apron and chef's hat, officiating.

Everyone had lounged about eating chops and sausages and some of those delicious chicken burgers that he'd ordered from the butcher in Hilbury. Her mouth was watering at the thought.

But in spite of the wording this sounded as if it would be a more formal event because it had a serious purpose. Cameron's departure. A celebration? No, for all Cameron's flippancy about his brother she believed that Grant would miss him and was sorry he was going.

There was a lump in her throat and the words on the card danced before her eyes. Cameron was going away.

She propped it up in front of her and

190

helped herself to one of the Mellstone Moments.

Cameron was right. Her day had been tiring. But her days were often tiring. The difference was the invitation to the party. She would see him again.

She hadn't really expected that she could change Hilda's mind. What was bothering her was Cameron knowing she hadn't even tried. But he had admitted that doing so would have been a waste of time, hadn't he? Yes, of course he had. He hadn't intended a criticism of her at all.

An early start next morning meant that carrot and coriander soup was bubbling away in a pan alongside one of butternut squash and ginger by the time five cars were in the gallery car park and the Shenston Scramblers busy pulling on hiking boots and checking maps ready for the off.

When 19 walkers piled into the tearoom laughing and talking, three hours later, Alix was glad of Saskia's help. And Tess Hartland had agreed to do extra hours in the showroom. Afterwards the three of them met in the kitchen for a restorative cup of tea. Then back to the showroom for Tess just in case anyone else showed up.

'All right for some.' Saskia's tone was bitter and this was a surprise after her friendly light-heartedness earlier that had pleased their customers. Tess had done well with the sale of many of Jenny's small pots and some larger ones, too. Everything had gone well.

Alix had her back to Saskia as she piled crockery into the dishwasher. Now she turned, a soup ladle in her hand.

'What's wrong, Saskia? You're not worried about your mother? How's Jenny today?'

Saskia hesitated.

'It's not like Mum to want to stay in bed. Yesterday she got up but not today.'

'I thought I'd call in and see her later,' Alix said.

'Mmm. Not sure. All she wants to do is sleep . . . '

Alix stared down at the soup ladle. Then she carefully placed it in the dishwasher and stood up.

'It's quiet here now, Saskia. You should go home and see how she is.'

Saskia shrugged.

'No rush.'

'Please, Saskia, go.'

Saskia hesitated but not for long.

'If you're sure?'

'I'm sure. And thanks for your help. You've been great but I can manage now.'

Saskia's quick smile vanished and as she went out through the back door on to the patio, her shoulders slumped.

*　*　*

Cameron's Land Rover wasn't parked in its usual place. Alix gazed at the space on the other side of the lane that now looked bereft. Someone had swept away the loose dust and cut back the overhanging thistles so that it looked larger now. She opened her garden gate and was halfway up the path when her phone rang.

'Alix?'

She let her bag slide to the ground. She didn't recognise the number. Her father's voice sounded strange.

'Dad?'

'I want Lois to have a word with you. Here she is.'

Typical Dad, dropping them both in it so suddenly with not a word of greeting.

'Hello?' Alix said breathlessly.

'Is this a good moment for you, my dear?' The voice was low and pleasant.

'Yes, yes, I think so.'

'It's your father.'

'Is he all right?'

'Never better, except for his sudden burst of conscience. I don't know quite what it's all about. Something to do with the sharing of the profits from the sale of your home with you, I think. He wants you to know that he won't force you to agree to sell but the money could be useful to both of you. He wanted me to tell you that.'

'Thank you, but I don't quite see . . .'

Alix looked round wildly at the tangled garden and saw that a shaft of late afternoon sunshine was highlighting the tips of the yellow buds on the climbing rose. This was as difficult for Lois as it was for herself, she thought. How much had Dad told her?

She felt she didn't know him any more, her self-contained father who had thought nothing of leaving his past behind him and going off alone because that was the way he wanted it.

Lois's voice softened.

'I hear you are settling well in Mellstone, Alix, making friends and so on. Please don't worry about your dad, my dear. He wants to do the best for everyone but doesn't always know what it is. But it's going to take a while to put your home on the market whatever he says and there'll be plenty of time for you to go down later when it's convenient for you.'

'It's just my brother's things . . . '

'I understand. I promise to make sure that nothing happens to them and they'll be kept safely for you.'

'Thank you.' Alix's tone was heartfelt. Lois had understood the importance to her of Olaf's belongings, few as they were — his binoculars, books . . . She struggled to visualise his untidy bed-room.

'You'll have my number now after this call,' Lois continued. 'Please phone me at any time if you're worried about anything.'

Alix stared at her phone as the call ended. She still didn't understand exactly what was going on about the cottage but Olaf's things would be safe for her. Lois had promised. She had to trust her.

Change of Plan

Alix averted her gaze from the car-less space on the other side of the lane as she took the track that led to the top of the downs. She hadn't come this way for some weeks, avoiding it because it reminded her of Cameron's harsh criticism of Olaf. But that wasn't the uppermost thought in her mind now as she reached the top of the track where the hedges fell away and she could gaze out across the distant vale.

Here she was close to the place where she and Dad had walked before he set out on his travels and she had started her new life here in Mellstone.

They had driven up to north Dorset from Cornwall that morning.

'I'll say goodbye to you somewhere up there,' her father said earlier as they approached the village and saw the rounded hills beyond. 'I can do with a bit of a breather.'

He meant that he hated being confined in any space at all and especially a car . . . this car, in fact, because it had belonged to his son. She, on the other hand, treasured it for that very reason. And so they had walked across the sheep-nibbled turf to get a view of the vale stretching into the azure distance. She had shivered, longing momentarily for the smell of seaweed and the shriek of wheeling sea birds they had left behind.

'Cold?' Dad's voice had sounded subdued when the moment came to say goodbye. He stood beside her, hunched against the chill breeze.

'I'll be all right, Dad.'

'That's my girl. Seen enough now?'

She nodded.

'Time's getting on.'

For a moment Dad gazed at her when they reached the car and then he caught her to him in a hug.

'You're too thin, my girl. Get some weight back on.'

'I will,' she promised, her voice muffled.

'Then I'll be off.'

He had yanked open the car door, pulled out his rucksack and hoisted it high on his back.

When he was no longer in sight she had got behind the wheel and driven the steep lane to Mellstone.

She had felt free and uncluttered then as Dad must have done too as he prepared to set off for the unknown. She had thought that he was deliberately leaving memories of Olaf behind and thinking only of himself.

But was that fair? Dad had always supported Olaf in an unobtrusive way. He had found the position of warden at the bird sanctuary that Olaf was delighted to accept. Were those the actions of a self-centred man? She stood quite still for a moment, thinking hard. In the distance a sheep bleated.

Couldn't it be true that Dad held memories of his son, Olaf, deep within himself to go with him wherever he was, just as her memories would always be with her? Humbled, Alix accepted this now as the truth.

By the same token, he had looked out for her, too. And how fortunate she had been that Hilda Lunt had allowed Jenny the free use of the cottage so that accommodation was provided not far from the gallery. But poor Hilda was living in that barn of a place that couldn't provide enough finance to do what her brother suggested. Unity Cottage, so perfect for them, wouldn't be on the market for ever.

She reached the viewpoint to look down on the village as she had done with Dad. This time she could pick out Meadowlands in which she had settled so well.

She thought of her cottage home near the clifftop in Cornwall that Dad wished to sell. Because of her, he hesitated to do so even though he needed the money now his circumstances had changed.

Saskia, who belonged to Mellstone, loved the tearoom as much if not more than she did herself and longed for it to be her concern.

Hilda needed to sell the Meadowlands

cottage to provide some of the finance needed for the purchase of Unity Cottage.

Her own good fortune was at the expense of others and that wasn't right. She wanted Dad to be proud of her but what good was that if she couldn't be proud of herself?

Alix kicked a loose clod of turf to one side of the sheep path she was on, reminded suddenly of seeing the mud on her back door when she had first arrived at the cottage. It had amused her to imagine the then unknown Cameron throwing it in retaliation for a similar attack by Hilda, prepared to fight back.

She must fight back in a different way and find the courage to make the right decision.

It sounded simple. Too simple.

* * *

A few days later Jenny was feeling better and insisted on being back at her wheel again.

'I'm never happier than doing this,' she

told Alix at coffee time when she emerged with fresh clay stains on her work apron and a patch of it on her forehead where she had pushed her hair back from her face.

Jenny laughed when Alix pointed this out and sounded so much like her normal self that Alix didn't mention the whole week off that the doctor had ordered but asked after her ankle instead.

Jenny held out her foot.

'See, the swelling's gone down.'

'But does it hurt still?'

'Nothing I can't cope with, sitting on my stool.'

She was back in her workshop again when a visitor arrived in the tearoom. The young woman, fair-haired and slim, was looking about her as if she was anxious to see someone and didn't quite know where she was.

Alix smiled a greeting.

'Can I help you?'

'I'm looking for Jenny Finlay. Is she here?'

'Not far away. I'll get her, shall I?'

'I don't want to be a nuisance. I know it's her first day back at work. Her daughter told me. I called at Marigold Cottage first. I'm Faith Varley, Cathy's daughter-in-law.'

Alix gestured towards one of the empty tables.

'Won't you sit down while I go and see if it's convenient? I won't be long.'

The door between the showroom and the workshop stood open so that Jenny was able to keep a watch as she worked. She looked up in surprise as Alix joined her.

'Something wrong?'

'Someone to see you. Fair-haired and not much older than me. Faith Varley, she said she was. They're home now, aren't they, she and her husband? She thought you'd be at home. Saskia told her where you were.'

Jenny looked alarmed.

'Saskia did? Right, I'll come at once. Bring us both coffee, will you please, Alix? No, wait a minute. Bring Faith in here.'

'In your workshop?'

'And the coffee, too. Best to let her see I'm busy. Just in case.'

In case of what? Alix wondered as she did as she was asked.

* * *

Jenny was surprised by what she had said, too, but she felt mistress of her domain in here, secure and in control. What did she expect of Faith . . . that she would lunge at her across the coffee? Ridiculous.

It was Saskia's reaction that had been the worry. She knew her daughter's long-held grudges only too well but she didn't know exactly how she still felt after being cast aside by Cathy's son, Oliver, six years ago when she discovered that it was her mother and not herself Oliver had wanted.

If only Saskia had tired of Mellstone in the weeks she had been here and moved on elsewhere out of harm's way.

Faith came in, looking around her in

a cautious way as if she was aware that she was intruding but didn't quite know what to do about it.

'Miss Finlay . . . Jenny?'

Jenny smiled as she dipped her hands in the sink to wash them.

'Some coffee's coming in a minute. You don't mind coming in here?'

'I saw your lovely work as I came through your showroom. Those subtle colours. I loved them.'

This was said so simply that Jenny warmed to her. Faith was a pretty girl in a fragile, gentle sort of way and quite different from the outgoing and practical-looking person she had pictured as Oliver's wife.

'I'd love to meet your twins,' she said impulsively.

Faith's smile was radiant.

'Cathy's looking after them this morning.'

'She's enjoying herself, then?'

'Very much so.'

The coffee arrived with a plate of Mellstone Moments.

'Let's find somewhere to sit,' Jenny said as she took the tray from Alix and with her foot hooked out a small paint-smeared table on which to put it. There was a stool in the corner and a folding chair nearby. 'These'll do.'

There was talk of the twins at first and then of Saskia who had directed Faith to the gallery. Faith spoke pleasantly of her, admiring the way Saskia was dressed in short skirt and pretty top. She looked down ruefully at her old jeans and jumper that had obviously seen better days.

'Was she, did she . . . ' Jenny paused, not knowing quite how to ask, merely wanting to know that there weren't any hard feelings between the two of them.

'She asked me in,' Faith said, 'but I said I was in a hurry. Maybe another time, she said.'

Relieved, Jenny nodded. She poured coffee and offered the Mellstone Moments.

Faith took one.

'I came because of Cathy. She was afraid to come herself.'

'Cathy, afraid?'

'A little.'

'Never. We've been good friends for years. Why would she be afraid?'

Faith leaned forward.

'She's worried because her daughter doesn't need you now to do the flowers for their wedding.'

'Why not? They've found someone else?'

'No, no, nothing like that.' Faith took a deep breath. 'They've had a secret wedding.'

'They eloped?'

'Not quite that. They arranged it without telling anybody, just went off one day and did it.'

'But why?'

'To save a lot of fuss, they said — and expense.'

'But Ralph . . . '

'Yes, I know. He wouldn't have minded how much it cost but they developed guilty consciences all of a sudden and just went ahead.'

'Poor Cathy. And Ralph.'

'We got married in Burkino Faso,'

Faith said sadly. 'They couldn't come to that wedding, either.'

Jenny was silent for a moment. Then she picked up her coffee cup and drained it. Cathy had been loving all the excitement and now there was nothing . . . well, nothing to plan for, to think about.

Faith was looking anxious now, her coffee untouched. She picked up a teaspoon, looked at it intently and then put if down again.

'Cathy was concerned that you would be upset at the financial loss to your business, you see. It was clear that it was beginning to make her ill so I thought it was best to come and tell you for her.'

Touched, Jenny smiled.

'It was kind of you, Faith. But, please there's no need for her to worry. I've got as much floristry work as I can handle anyway. It's fine by me, really.'

'I'm so glad.' Faith looked happier now as she picked up her coffee cup. She listened to Jenny's account of the flower-arranging side of her business with interest.

'I was pleased to be asked to take charge of the flowers for Felicity,' Jenny said. 'Who wouldn't be? But be sure to tell Cathy that I'm happy this way, too. I hear that you and Oliver are thinking of moving back to this country permanently?'

'Oh, yes.' Faith's eyes lit up. 'We've been thinking about for a long time. It's something we both want.'

'His parents will be pleased.'

'He's having a long chat with his father now. Or he was. Here he is now!'

Faith half-rose in her seat as Oliver came in. A brief smile for his wife and then he turned to Jenny.

'Jenny! Good to see you again.'

She sprang up to greet him and for a long moment he held her hand in both of his before releasing it.

'And you, Oliver.'

His hair was shorter than when he was last home about 11 months ago. He seemed broader too, unless it was because of the bulky clothes he was wearing that were even rougher than Faith's.

Seeing Jenny looking at them, he laughed.

'Not looking my best, I know, but I've been helping Dad clear out the barn and it's filthy work.'

'Getting some practice in for when you come back for good?'

'Someone's been talking. Mum?'

'She has your interests at heart.'

Oliver laughed.

'Even she understands that working for Dad full time is not one of them.' He glanced at his wife. 'The first priority for us is finding somewhere to live.'

'And that we can afford,' Faith added.

'Our plans are a bit vague at the moment but you can be sure some sort of charity work is involved. I'll be working from home, too, on a project I'm involved in so we'll need a bit of space.'

Faith gave her gentle smile.

'We'll be caring for disadvantaged people, you see. My parents will help as much as they can but . . . ' She looked helplessly at Oliver who responded with a shrug.

'We'd like somewhere in need of renovation,' he said. 'Falling apart, with luck.'

'We're good at getting stuck in physically,' Faith said.

Oliver smiled at Jenny.

'But not when we're loitering here, however pleasantly. Let's get going, Faith.'

Jenny got to her feet again.

'I haven't even offered you coffee, Oliver.'

'Not to worry. We're interrupting your work.'

'Not a bit of it. It can wait. You'll convince Cathy that I'm not plunged into despair?'

Oliver laughed.

'We'll do our best.'

'And I congratulate the happy couple for taking charge of their lives.'

'But better if they could have done it sooner?'

'Well, maybe, but I'm happy for them. And tell your mother I'll be along to see her this evening.'

'Will do. She'll be glad to see you.

She's babysitting the twins now while we search the area for our perfect home.'

Jenny laughed.

'And you're suitably dressed for the kind of place you're after.'

'Well spotted. Maybe we should go home and change first, Faith?'

She looked at him with her sweet smile.

As they left, lingering a little in the doorway, Oliver looked back over his shoulder. His grin was infectious and Jenny found herself smiling too as she returned to her wheel and placed a large lump of wet clay on it.

Saskia's dreaded meeting with Faith had gone smoothly, in a friendly way, even. Dreaded by herself, of course, when she awoke with depressing thoughts in the middle of the night. She smiled ruefully. It seemed that Saskia was growing up at last and she was thankful.

A Kiss in the Darkness

There were fewer people at Cameron's leaving party than at the barbecue which was just as well, Alix thought, as she accepted a glass of chilled fruit punch from Grant. Even so, the small room was overflowing.

With streams of rain sliding down the window panes outside and the hint of an early dusk the garden was out of the question.

Cameron, joining her a few moments later, looked at the glass in her hand.

'Is that the best you can manage?'

'For the moment, yes. The night is young.'

'The drink might run out.'

She glanced at the laden table pushed against the wall.

'I don't think there's any chance of that.'

She had tried to slip into the room

unnoticed but moments later he was with her, turning his back on a rowdy group containing Michelle telling some joke that had the others falling about in mirth.

'This isn't quite your scene, is it?' he said.

'Or yours?'

'Grant thinks it's up to him to do it for my sake so I play along, the dear old boy.' His words sounded offhand but she knew better. The brothers would miss each other and this was as good a way as any to put a brave face on it.

'Give me open spaces any day,' he added.

'And you'll soon be getting those.' In under 48 hours, she thought. She gripped the stem of her glass tightly.

'One of us will be out of here anyway. Hilda will be pleased.'

'If she knows about it.'

'She knows all right. Grant told her.'

Alix was surprised.

'He's seen her?'

'She summoned him to call on her

yesterday. Don't ask me why.' He glanced away from her as if he had noticed something on the far wall but then decided he was wrong.

'And they didn't come to blows?'

'Not as far as I know. I might get more out of him tomorrow. He knows I want to find something before I leave that's rather rare. He's agreed to come with me to the coast. One of his better ideas.' He hesitated for a moment, looked wildly round again. 'This rain could scupper everything,' he added.

Alix wondered what he had in mind but before she could ask, Cameron was claimed by another vociferous group.

Left to her own devices, Alix moved to the kitchen, thinking to replenish her empty glass with tap water. She had no heart for anything stronger at the moment. Or for food, either, come to that.

It looked as if Grant had all that in hand. Several catering boxes were lined up on the table. She was tempted to open them and arrange the contents on the plates and dishes left handy nearby.

Paper ones, she noticed, promising a limited need of washing-up at the end of the evening. But her interference might not be welcome, even if it was her day job to cater to people's needs.

Alix jumped, startled, as the phone on the wall rang. The noise from the adjoining room was so high that she wondered that anyone heard but Grant came at once, smiling in apology at her as he lifted the receiver.

He waved at her to stay where she was.

'Only excuses from a late-comer, no doubt,' he mouthed.

But by his expression it seemed far more serious and she began to move towards the door. He replaced the receiver and looked helplessly at the boxes on the table.

'Would you like me to help you with all these?' she said.

His face cleared.

'Please. Michelle's supposed to be in charge here but if you don't mind . . .You won't yatter on all the time, anyway. I don't think I could bear that.'

'Leave it to me, Grant.' She could see that he was in no fit state to concentrate on anything much.

Inside the boxes were a variety of sandwiches, small meat pies, chicken drumsticks coated in something shiny, slices of smoked salmon on brown bread and sausage rolls. Good solid party food, she thought, and easy to cope with in crowded conditions.

'Get someone sensible to help pass them round, would you?' he said. 'The show must go on.'

'Bad news?'

He nodded.

'Cameron mustn't know yet.'

'Mustn't know what?' a voice said from the doorway.

She picked up a dish of sandwiches and escaped. By the time she had handed it around and found Saskia to help with the rest there was silence from the kitchen and then both Grant and Cameron were back among them. Both looked strained but Grant was holding himself rigid and his face was pale.

The evening wore on. People were beginning to leave now, saying their farewells and hugging and kissing both Grant and Cameron. Alix stood a little to one side, knowing that it had come to the moment she dreaded.

Cameron stepped towards her.

'There's all the food to be finished up.'

'No, I couldn't, really . . . '

'Why not, lass? You've eaten nowt all evening. You look fair starved.' His attempt at a Yorkshire accent was laughable but she didn't feel like laughing.

Saskia appeared then together with Tess and Nigel Hartland who were walking her home. It would have been easy for Alix to slip away with them but she stayed where she was, despising herself for not doing the sensible thing.

'Get to bed,' Cameron said to Grant as the room began to empty. 'I'll see you in the morning.' He turned to Alix when he had gone. 'That phone call gave him a shock. He's just heard that his ex-colleague has died. The funeral's tomorrow in Chichester.'

'And he has to go?'

'No question.'

'And he minds about letting you down?'

'That, too. But that's not important. The finding of some insignificant little flower compared with the death of anyone? No contest, surely?'

Of course there wasn't. No contest at all. Cameron could go on his own in pursuit of whatever it was.

'Shall I help you clear up here or would you rather be on your own?' She hated to see Cameron so downcast.

He shook his head.

'I'll be fine. You go on home.'

She longed to give him a hug but it wouldn't do. She must keep something of her dignity intact.

He pulled out his phone and tested the torchlight on it.

'I'll see you to your door.'

'There's no need, really.'

'Get going, girl.'

She led the way down the path with his torchlight shining before her, acutely aware of him behind her. At her own gate she had her phone out too.

'I can manage now.'

'But I can't,' he said, his voice husky.

She turned to face him and the next moment she was in his arms. In the sudden darkness she felt the warmth of his body as he bent his head and kissed her.

'There,' he said, releasing her. 'I shall never forget you, Alix.'

She moved back a little.

'I'm sorry about tomorrow,' she said impulsively.

'How sorry?' There was hope in his voice. 'Any chance of you coming with me? Winspit to Dancing Ledge.'

'Ledge?' she said doubtfully.

'There's poetry in those names, don't you think? A beautiful part of the south Dorset coast on the cliffs, about thirty-five miles or so south from here and a pretty ride to get there.'

She didn't doubt it but she hesitated. The word ledge was worrying.

'What will we be looking for?' she said.

He let out the breath he had been holding.

'Something so insignificant it might be hard to find. The early gentian, a tiny mauve flower and difficult to locate amongst the grass because it only opens in bright weather. It's only found in the UK and mainly in Dorset on chalk and limestone and that area's the most likely. I'm hoping the forecast is good for tomorrow.'

'I'll come.'

'You will?' His voice lightened. 'You're quite sure about that?'

The last chance of a day in his company? Of course she was sure. Her heart quickened as she thought of it.

'An early start?'

'Definitely. We'll make the most of the day. A meal out afterwards, of course. Why not?'

'It sounds good.' Practical issues

could be taken care of. it wasn't too late to phone Saskia. Jenny wouldn't mind her taking over in the tearoom in the circumstances. The thoughts flashed through Alix's mind in an instant.

She smiled although she knew he couldn't see.

'I'll be ready.'

Light on the Horizon?

The hazy downs receded swiftly behind them as they set out next day. Ahead, the grey sky above the horizon was spreading rapidly over what little blue sky was left.

Alix settled back in her seat, anxious now about arriving at the place Cameron talked about with so much enthusiasm.

'A Purbeck village,' he said. 'Lovely stone buildings, handy pub and a car park. What more could we want?'

'A sunny day?'

He smiled.

'You want it all.'

'Don't you, Cameron?'

'I might do, but I don't always get it.'

She didn't, either, but how fortunate she was to get this last chance to spend a day in Cameron's company. He was so keen to discover this rare little flower that she was enthusiastic about it, too, even though it was most likely to grow near cliff edges in this part of Dorset.

Cameron glanced sideways at her and she managed a smile. It wasn't the village among the Purbeck Hills that alarmed her but the cliffs less than a mile away and the path near the edge with the sea swirling below. The tight feeling in her chest was already beginning to grow as they reached Stourford's bypass but she had to control it.

She had been unable to cope with the view of the cliffs from their cottage window because of the traumatic memories they held. Maybe this would help to cure her so that she felt able to return to Cornwall soon to help clear the cottage for its eventual sale.

They arrived at Worth Hinton all too soon but not soon enough for Cameron, it seemed. His boots were on and laced up almost before she had taken hers out of their bag.

He slung the strap on his binoculars round his neck, shouldered his camera and then grinned at her.

'Anyone would think you didn't want to come with me.' Then, suddenly, he was serious. 'Sorry, Alix, that was crass of me. Put it down to excitement at the thrill of discovery.'

She nodded and concentrated on her footwear, carefully placing her trainers in the bag and storing it in the boot. The lid slammed down harder than she intended.

'Sorry, I didn't mean . . . '

'I'll look after you.'

She didn't doubt it. Far better than she had looked after Olaf, anyway.

'Yes, yes, I know.'

'Come on then. Best foot forward.'

Heads down before the rising wind, they set out, at first on the road and then on tracks between stone wails. Eventually Cameron paused and opened a field gate for her to go ahead of him. It clanged shut behind them.

They could see the sea now, grey and ominous. Cameron paused and held his binoculars to his eyes.

'We'll catch sight of puffins presently,

with luck. We're heading down to Winspit on the coast path and then along to Dancing Ledge where's there's a colony of them. Yes, look, there's a couple now flying out to sea.'

He passed the binoculars to her but by the time she had adjusted them the birds were gone.

'Not to worry,' he said, taking the binoculars back. 'From Winspit along to Dancing Ledge is about a mile and a half. There'll be plenty more chances.'

There were those magical names again, but to Alix they meant cliffs and surging sea. She wished she could think of them without this flutter of apprehension.

'On a day like this there shouldn't be hordes of people at Dancing Ledge when we get there,' he said. 'I'd like you to see it in ail its wild glory. Not that I'm anti-social but sometimes it's good to have a place to yourself for a little while at least.'

She agreed.

'To create the right atmosphere.'

'Got it in one.'

There was plenty of atmosphere here already with the gloomy sky and the haunting cries of distant sea birds. On the slopes ahead of them were the strip lynchets. These were the long narrow terraces that she knew dated from the days of mediaeval farming. She liked the feeling of age and of time passing with little change.

On they went. Cameron was using his camera instead of binoculars now. His pleasure in finding early spider-orchids in the grass was catching.

On they went again until they reached the coast path. She tried not to look at the cliff edge or at the sea that was much rougher and closer than she liked.

There were signs around here that once this area had been used for quarry-ing, the workings long overgrown with grass and thistles. And wild flowers, too, of course, lurking among them. She rec-ognised small blue forget-me-knots, thrift and more wild orchids, different from the spider one.

As they headed east Cameron told her of another old quarry at Dancing Ledge and the rough steps down between the rocks to a flat area below.

'Believe it or not, there's an old swimming pool there, blasted out of the rock.'

'A swimming pool?'

'Used by a local school long ago but disused now.'

'Incredible.'

'Isn't it just?'

But it seemed there were many flowers he wished to photograph first. Alix waited, holding herself stiffly and saying nothing when Cameron found a short way down the cliff a little way ahead and indicated with a wave of his hand that he wouldn't be long.

She took a deep breath and then couldn't see him. She waited, her mouth dry. Moments passed. She took a step forward and looked over the edge. He wasn't far down but he was bent over, leaning out away from her.

She bit back a cry.

He straightened and looked up her. 'Anything wrong?'

'No, no!' And of course there wasn't. His path went no further. He was perfectly safe. He hadn't leaned too far. She could see that now.

Olaf would have known of the danger he had been in but had chosen to ignore it. The tight knot of guilt deep down inside her began to lessen a little. She breathed deeply to calm herself.

A few moments more and Cameron climbed back up to join her. He replaced his camera in its bag which he slung over one shoulder.

'All right now?'

Weak with relief, she nodded.

'Sorry. I only meant to be a moment.'

'It's all right. I know that.' But her hands were shaking.

He took hold of them.

'You're cold.'

'I'll soon warm up when we get going again.'

The light was dimmer now. Black clouds were forming over the sea and coming swiftly towards them.

He frowned.

'That looks bad.'

Before they could move the storm erupted with a suddenness that was breathtaking. He pulled her back against a rock that offered little shelter. Ahead of them the path was obliterated in seconds by the slanting rain. Sheets of water cascaded over them. They were wet through.

'Not what I was expecting,' he said as the rain eased.

'Me neither.'

She rubbed her arm across her face in a vain attempt to dry it. Away from their ineffectual shelter, Cameron shook himself and then looked at her in concern.

'A drowned rat,' she said.

'You can still smile?'

'Only just.'

'That's more than I can, fool that I was. I should have seen it coming in time to head for proper shelter.'

'But it's stopping now.'

And so it was. Water dripped around them but the path was still slimy with mud. Cameron glanced ahead at the pools of water that blocked it and looked as if they were there to stay.

'We'd better call it a day.'

'But we can't. What about your little mauve flower, the early gentian?'

'I've photographed other flowers. That will do.'

'But a bit longer won't make much difference.'

A steely hint of light on the horizon seemed a good omen.

He followed her gaze.

'Not enough, I'm afraid. The early gentian needs full sunshine to dry it out and even then might not open. In any case the path ahead is blocked, as far as I can see.'

He sounded determined, amused even, but still she remonstrated until he cut her short.

'Come, Alix, be sensible and not like Hilda when she's made up her mind about something. How sensible is it of her to insist on selling your Meadow-lands cottage to my brother there and then, take it or leave it?'

'What?'

Cameron stopped and swung round to face Alix.

'You didn't know? Oh, Alix, I'm so sorry to blurt it out like that. She swore Grant to secrecy. I heard, most of it, and assumed she had already told you and you had worked something out with Jenny.'

'When was this?'

'When she demanded an audience with Grant. He had to make an instant decision. If he didn't agree to purchase your place there and then she'd take it off the market and that would be that.'

Surprised into silence, Alix could only stare at him.

Cameron's voice was tight.

'I'm so sorry, Alix, so very sorry.'

'So what did Grant do?' she said at last.

'What else could he do? He doesn't like the way it's done and I don't either.

But Alix, I know he wouldn't throw you out. He could put his plans to modernise on hold.'

She shivered.

'But what made Hilda change her mind?' A trickle of water ran down her face but she took no notice. He rubbed it away for her so gently she hardly felt it.

'Astonishing, I agree.'

She was silent again, thinking that even if Grant agreed to let her remain in the Meadowlands cottage for the time being he would need to charge rent and that would make things difficult for her. For Jenny, too, who couldn't be expected to pay for her accommodation or to raise her salary to meet it. In any case, if the cottage belonged to him then who was she to stand in the way of his plans for it?

The light on the horizon was gone now and the sea dull.

'Now,' Cameron said, 'look at those black clouds. More rain's coming. Run.'

Alix kept as close behind Cameron as

possible and had no more time to think. The rain came again as they squelched their way up the field and through the gate on to a track that was now slimy with mud.

They arrived at his vehicle and she leaned against it, gasping. He pulled open the door and helped her inside.

He climbed into the driver's seat, wiping his face with the car duster and leaving a smear of mud on his forehead.

'What a day! I've failed miserably and ruined yours, too.' He put his vehicle into gear and they set off at speed. 'The sooner I get you home the better before you expire with cold.'

'It's been a good day for me,' she said in a low voice.

'You're a girl in a million putting up with all that. And then the shock of learning of Hilda's sudden decision. There isn't much time to make it up to you.'

'You don't have to make up anything, Cameron.'

'Oh, I think I do.'

The windscreen wipers were doing a sterling job and she stared at them, mesmerised. The day wasn't a failure for her because she had at last come to terms with something important. But it wasn't enough, not nearly enough.

Cameron faced change, big time. Dad chose change. A challenge for both of them and they were going forward into the future with confidence.

Hilda's dilapidated home would go on the market as well and there might be somebody interested in a run-down property ripe for improvements. Cathy's son and daughter-in-law? Who knew?

Hilda would set up home with her brother in Unity Cottage, to the benefit of both. Hilda was the only one who hadn't made a choice.

But she, Alix, had chosen to accept the job in Mellstone even if it had been found for her. She had a car. There was the money Dad seemed to think was hers on the sale of their old home. This would make it possible for her to find other accommodation in reach of Mellstone.

There was no problem with that.

And yet the ache of something not quite right was still there. She closed her eyes, listening to swish of water on the road and the dull thud of rain on the car roof.

* * *

A hot shower, hot soup from a packet stored for an emergency and Alix felt a lot better. She finished her meal and carried her plate and mug to the draining board.

Her wet clothes, soaking in the sink, needed to be dealt with first. The rain had eased off again now but the drips from the thatch still fell in rhythmic patterns on to the ground outside. A watery sunlight shone fitfully on the cobbles of the yard.

She wondered how Saskia was coping with the wet day and the likely absence of customers. More Mellstone Moments being made? Anxious to find out, Alix took down her best jacket from the hook near the back door and slipped her feet into her trainers.

The smell of herbs and onion greeted her as she opened the outside door at the gallery and went through to the kitchen.

Saskia was startled to see her.

'How have things been here?' Alix asked. Saskia frowned.

'No-one's been in. No surprise on a day like this. I had to do something and Mum thought you wouldn't mind me doing some experimenting. She'll be here in a minute.'

'Are you going to tell me what you've got in the oven,' Alix asked, 'or just keep it for a lovely surprise?'

'I've used all sorts of different fillings,' Saskia said apologetically. 'It seemed a good idea at the time.'

'I can't argue with that.'

But it wasn't until Jenny arrived, surprised to see Alix too, that Saskia risked opening the oven door and stood back at the rush of steamy air. Inside were two trays each containing four round dishes the size of small saucers. She lifted them out with care and placed them on a heat-proof mat on the table.

'Individual quiches,' she said proudly. 'Each one with a different filling.'

'Lucky I haven't eaten yet,' Jenny said. 'I'd have been here earlier but Hilda called to see me with some disturbing news.'

'It usually is if Hilda's involved,' Saskia muttered.

Ignoring her, Jenny looked at Alix who spoke quickly.

'I know about it already, Jenny. I was coming to see you. It'll all work out, I promise.'

'Oh, my dear, I don't know what to say.' Alix smiled at her.

'Please don't worry. I'll sort something out.'

Alix turned her attention to the quiches but then looked up at the sound of the outside door opening.

Jenny looked startled.

'Late customers? I'd better get back to the showroom.'

But there was no need. Earlier, Cameron had looked like someone res-cued from a wrecked ship but now in his bright jersey and with his hair dry and brushed back from his forehead he looked a new man.

'Food?' he said with interest.

'Something to try out,' Saskia said. 'I've been experimenting. You can join in, if you like.'

He smiled in apology.

'Sorry. I've something on the agenda and need Alix with me. Come on, Alix, we're going somewhere.'

End of the Rainbow

The haste with which Cameron got her outside was remarkable.

'A pub at Shilling End,' he said as they closed the door behind them. 'How does that sound? A log fire later this evening. I checked. Will you come? My vehicle's outside.'

Bemused, she agreed.

'I've dried out my chariot as well as I could and the seats are fine. I've put towels on them just in case.' He sounded happier now, relieved even.

Alix looked straight ahead as they walked up the lane together to the top of the downs. The late afternoon was calm now, rain-washed and slightly cloudy but still with the hint that there was more rain to come.

But what did it matter? They would be indoors, seated by that log fire and she was going to enjoy every single moment and not think of what tomorrow would bring.

'I believe we should all appreciate the present moment,' he said as if he knew what she was thinking. 'It's all we have, after all.'

'True, the present moment,' she said, lingering over the words.

'The past relegated to the past? Do you really mean it, Alix?'

He was more solemn than she had seen him and she knew that this moment was important to him. It was for her too.

She smiled.

'Memories, good ones as well as bad.'

He nodded, satisfied.

'We know what has already passed.'

'And we know what's in the present. But that's all.'

'Wise girl, knowing we can't see into the future.'

'But at least I know we're going to Shilling End. I don't know what it's like because I've never been there before. I can't visualise it.'

He laughed.

'Now you're making fun of me.'

'Never.' She laughed, too.

'There's something I want to show you first. Are you game?'

'Why not?'

'It isn't far off our route.' He pulled into a layby and switched off the engine, walked round to the passenger door and offered her his hand.

'I can't wait any longer,' he said, gently pulling her to her feet.

His arms were round her and she leaned against him, her heart full. His kiss was gentle at first but then more passionate and she could hardly bear it when it stopped and the spell was momentarily broken.

'I want to take you to that hillock over there,' he said suddenly with the solemnity that hadn't quite left him.

'What for?' she said.

'This is important to me.'

It certainly seemed so from the intent expression on his face. She knew that the hillock in question was one of the prehistoric burial mounds that Grant had suggested his group might be interested in, along with others in the area. Cameron had always scorned such things, but not now, it seemed.

They reached the grassy mound and Cameron knelt down to cup his hands round a specimen so tiny it was hard to pick out.

'See here?'

She crouched down beside him. The minute flower was hard see in the long wet grass.

'Remember earlier, Alix, when we were setting out for Dancing Ledge?'

'As if I could forget.'

'This little plant is growing here in a place I would never have dreamed of finding it. I came across it the other day.' He smiled.

'But that's not the early gentian we were looking for?'

'I was hoping to find that earlier, it's true. But now there's this, the lesser heart's-ease.'

Alix still felt a loss.

'It's lovely,' she said as they got to their feet, 'but I wish we could have carried on making our way along the cliff path in search of the rare one you had set your heart on.'

'And I wish the day hadn't been such a disaster for you.'

'A disaster, never!' she said with passion. 'The cliffs and the surging sea don't hold any terror for me now. I've learned that today. You've done that for me, Cameron, and I'm grateful.

'You see, I need to go back to Cornwall for a few days soon for Dad's sake,' she continued, 'and now when I'm there I shall walk along the cliff path and think of the happy times Olaf and I had together.'

'Which no-one can take away from you.'

She smiled, pleased that he understood.

'I would like to see your old haunts one day,' Cameron said, 'and get to know the real Alix because of them.'

'The real Alix is here,' she said.

'Tomorrow I plan to go north, but

not to stay. I shall explain my decision not to take up the position after all.'

Alix stared at him, unable at first to take in what Cameron was saying. Suddenly she couldn't bear it.

'But what about those people you wanted to help? What about them?'

'One of the other applicants will be pleased to take over.'

'No, no, that can't be,' she burst out. 'The work you love, your wish to do what's best for the young people in your care to give them something of value to last them all their lives. You can't give that up. I won't let you.'

'Your happiness is important to me,' he said. 'You've made a life for yourself here now after a traumatic past and I salute you for it. This is your place, Alix, and I want to share it with you.'

'And your happiness to important to me. I would go anywhere in the world with you,' she said simply.

There was a second's stunned silence. She couldn't breathe for the rush of emotion.

He was looking at her in wonder.

'And does that include Nidderdale in North Yorkshire?'

She nodded.

'Of course.'

'But what of the tearoom?'

She thought of Saskia, eager to take over.

'I'll speak to Jenny.'

Dazed by happiness, nothing could surprise her, not even be lieving that it was the outpouring of her grief that had touched Hilda and made her see reason in her brother's plans.

'I think we might have got Hilda wrong,' she said.

Cameron's smile was radiant as he caught her to him and there was no quick release this time.

When at last they parted she saw that more clouds were mustering, some of them edged with narrow bands of gold.

She glanced to the south where she knew Dancing Ledge was, invisible, of course, at this distance. But in her imagination, she saw it. And something else too as she looked around her.

She caught her breath.

'Look, Cameron, a rainbow!'

His face shone with enthusiasm.

'A promise for the future,' he said, his voice husky.

Alix smiled. The rainbow was still there, brighter now if anything. The earth seemed a brighter place because of it, as together they watched it fade away.

His hand felt warm and comforting as they walked back together over the damp, sweet-smelling turf. In all this wide area he had found the lesser hearts-ease. And she had found heart's ease too in a totally different way.

'I know one thing about the future,' she said. 'We'll find that early gentian together one day.'

We do hope that you have enjoyed reading this large print book.

Did you know that all of our titles are available for purchase?

We publish a wide range of high quality large print books including:
Romances, Mysteries, Classics
General Fiction
Non Fiction and Westerns

Special interest titles available in large print are:
The Little Oxford Dictionary
Music Book, Song Book
Hymn Book, Service Book

Also available from us courtesy of Oxford University Press:
Young Readers' Dictionary
(large print edition)
Young Readers' Thesaurus
(large print edition)

For further information or a free brochure, please contact us at:
Ulverscroft Large Print Books Ltd.,
The Green, Bradgate Road, Anstey,
Leicester, LE7 7FU, England.
Tel: (00 44) **0116 236 4325**
Fax: (00 44) **0116 234 0205**

Other titles in the
Linford Romance Library:

DUKE IN DANGER

Fenella J. Miller

Lady Helena Faulkner agrees to marry only if her indulgent parents can find a gentleman who fits her exacting requirements. Wild and unconventional, she has no desire for romance, but wants a friend who will let her live as she pleases. Lord Christopher Drake, known to Helena as Kit, her brother's best friend, needs a rich wife to support his mother and siblings. It could be the perfect arrangement. But when malign forces do their best to separate them, can Helena and Kit overcome the disasters and find true happiness?

MY SUNSHINE

Anne Holman

Having escaped a controlling relationship, won the lottery and given up work, Jenny is adrift at twenty-nine. Then her landlady's widowed son Alexander seeks her help in a family emergency, and she is catapulted into a different world of muddy boots, wayward pets and three children in need of love and a firm hand. But Jenny is conflicted — to fall for Alexander means absorbing so much responsibility, and then there's his obvious uneasiness when it comes to her fortune. More importantly, do Alexander's feelings match her growing love for him?